KU-619-127

Mr Chartwell

Mr Chartwell

REBECCA HUNT

FIG TREE
an imprint of
PENGUIN BOOKS

FIG TREE

Published by the Penguin Group
Penguin Books Ltd, 80 Strand, London WC2R ORL, England
Penguin Group (USA) Inc., 375 Hudson Street, New York, New York 10014, USA
Penguin Group (Canada), 90 Eglinton Avenue East, Suite 700, Toronto, Ontario, Canada M4P 2Y3
(a division of Pearson Penguin Canada Inc.)
Penguin Ireland, 25 St Stephen's Green, Dublin 2, Ireland (a division of Penguin Books Ltd)
Penguin Group (Australia), 250 Camberwell Road, Camberwell, Victoria 3124, Australia
(a division of Pearson Australia Group Pty Ltd)
Penguin Books India Pvt Ltd, 11 Community Centre, Panchsheel Park, New Delhi – 110 017, India
Penguin Group (NZ), 67 Apollo Drive, Rosedale, North Shore 0632, New Zealand
(a division of Pearson New Zealand Ltd)
Penguin Books (South Africa) (Pty) Ltd, 24 Sturdee Avenue, Rosebank, Johannesburg 2196, South Africa

Penguin Books Ltd, Registered Offices: 80 Strand, London WC2R ORL, England

www.penguin.com

First published 2010

I

Copyright © Rebecca Hunt, 2010
The moral right of the author has been asserted

Extract from *Churchill: Strategy and History* by Tuvia Ben-Moshe: copyright © 1992 by
Lynne Rienner Publishers, Inc. Used with permission of the publisher
Extract from *Painting as Pastime* by Winston Churchill: reproduced with permission of
Curtis Brown Ltd, London, on behalf of The Estate of Winston Churchill
Extract from *Great Contemporaries* by Winston Churchill: reproduced with permission of Curtis Brown Ltd,
London, on behalf of The Estate of Winston Churchill, copyright © Winston S. Churchill

Every effort has been made to trace copyright holders and to obtain their permission for the use of copyright material.
The publisher apologizes for any errors or omissions and would be grateful to be notified of any corrections that
should be incorporated in future editions of this book.

All rights reserved
Without limiting the rights under copyright
reserved above, no part of this publication may be
reproduced, stored in or introduced into a retrieval system,
or transmitted, in any form or by any means (electronic, mechanical,
photocopying, recording or otherwise), without the prior
written permission of both the copyright owner and
the above publisher of this book

14.75pt Dante MT Std
Typeset by Palimpsest Book Production Limited, Falkirk, Stirlingshire
Printed in Great Britain by Clays Ltd, St Ives plc

A CIP catalogue record for this book is available from the British Library

HARDBACK ISBN: 978-1-905-49069-1
TRADE PAPERBACK ISBN: 978-1-905-49064-6

www.greenpenguin.co.uk

CLASS

FIHUN

BARCODE

LO8244WOS59

DATE

18 MAR 2011

SOUTH KENT COLLEGE
ASHFORD LEARNING CENTRE

Mixed Sources
Product group from well-managed
forests and other controlled sources
www.fsc.org Cert no. SA-COC-1592
© 1996 Forest Stewardship Council

Penguin Books is committed to a sustainable future
for our business, our readers and our planet.
The book in your hands is made from paper
certified by the Forest Stewardship Council.

This book is dedicated with love and thanks to my parents

Acknowledgements

A huge thank you to my friends and family, Sarah Lutyens, Juliet Annan and Susan Kamil.

And an extra special thank you to Simon Davison.

Wednesday 22 July 1964

I

5.30 a.m.

Winston Leonard Spencer Churchill's mouth was pursed as if he had a slice of lemon hidden in there. Now eighty-nine, he often woke early. Grey dawn appeared in a crack between the curtains, amassing the strength to invade. Churchill prepared himself for the day ahead, his mind putting out analytical fingers and then coming at the day in a fist, ready for it.

A view of the Weald of Kent stretched beyond the window, lying under an animal skin of mist. Bordered to the west by Crockham Hill and to the east by Toys Hill, Churchill's red-brick house sat in a shallow coomb, enclosed by a horseshoe of ancient forest that opened in a long, green horizon to the south.

Although fully awake, Churchill's eyes remained closed. On his back, the bedcovers pulled and folded at his waist, he lay with his arms alongside the quilted log of his body. On the other side of the house, Clementine lay sleeping in her four-poster bed. He thought of his wife, wishing to be with her.

But Churchill wasn't alone in his bedroom; something else in the dark, a mute bulk in the corner, a massive thing, was watching him with tortured concentration.

Churchill was aware of its presence. He didn't need to see or hear it to know it was there; he had more of a sense, an instinctual certainty when it appeared. Its eyes pressed on him hotly, imploring him to wake up. It willed him to move. After hours of waiting it ached with the desire to explode from the corner and shake him.

Churchill spoke in a barely audible whisper, not that it mattered – he knew the thing would be listening.

'Bugger off.'

There was a long silence as the thing scrabbled to compose itself. Churchill could feel it grinning filthily in the blackness. It said with unsuppressed relish, *'No.'*

2

8.30 a.m.

In a terraced house in Battersea, Esther Hammerhans came tearing down the stairs with one arm through a cardigan sleeve, the rest flapping at her legs, and turned off the hob. The kettle stopped its screaming and threw out hysterical clouds of steam. Esther found the teapot and filled it with hot water, some spilling over the work surface. The tea leaves had been forgotten, something she discovered five minutes later, after a wild campaign with the washing up. 'Idiots!' she cursed the tea leaves, beating them into the water with a spoon.

Then she put on the entire cardigan. This seemed a good step, a positive move. A moment passed where she calmed herself; it was important to look calm. Mr Chartwell would arrive at any minute; it was important that the first impression was a good one. She admired the yellow cabinet doors and drawers which she had scrubbed earlier, the walls painted a paler yellow and lit with a fluorescent tube on the ceiling. The dark orange tiled floor had been mopped, pots of spices and dried herbs arranged neatly on wiped white gloss shelves. The blue Formica-topped kitchen table was arranged with a vase of flowers, a stainless steel candlestick there for show as if she used it every day. Sugar cubes were stacked into the only small bowl without chips. A tasteless bowl designed to resemble a cockerel; Esther had hidden the cockerel-head lid in a drawer.

Esther went to the mirror hung near the window and examined herself, seeing a wispy, long-haired person with a delicate underbite.

She had always been slim, slimmer now and a bit bare with it. The mirror returned a smile which expressed fatigue, a varnish of melancholy painted behind the features. The general package, Esther decided, would not benefit from further examination.

The boxroom she wanted to rent didn't have many things but it did have a garden view. Light mobbed every crevice from the first gloss of daybreak, and this would flaunt the room's extreme cleanliness. The carpet, meticulously hoovered, had come up well and showed its brilliant ochre colour, the colour of a toy lion. A decorative earthenware tile hung on the wall above the bed – a painted scene of a hillside village in Greece, the white cottages whirling with violently green and orange foliage, thick black lines everywhere as if drawn with a thumb. Her friend Beth had loaned her a single bed, a very modest and old bed which didn't look so humble when dressed with fresh sheets and blankets. The light bulb was decorated with a woven wicker shade, purchased last week, which Esther felt gave the room a sense of style. A new wardrobe completed the room's transformation into a bedroom. If necessary she would throw in the occasional use of her car.

But – disappointment – only one note of interest had answered her advert, silently hand-delivered yesterday evening from a Mr Chartwell requesting a viewing in the morning. The lettering was savage and strange, pressed so hard into the paper the commas were torn through. It seemed to Esther this note had been written by someone deeply unfamiliar with a pen, someone who held it like a pole they wanted to bang into the ground. Finding the note, Esther had creased it in a fist, stunned suddenly at the idea of sharing her home, the thought of the intrusion making her gently seasick.

Maybe, thought Esther, now in the front room at the record player, she should put some music on to insinuate that she was a hip landlady as well as a calm one. Mr Chartwell was probably a music fan; he would appreciate the charts. The Rolling Stones were number one with 'It's All Over Now', and Esther had bought the single. She busied herself with this task, supremely confident. Placing the needle on the record, the song blared at an obscene volume, Mick Jagger's voice screaming through the tissues of her head. Esther snatched the needle off.

The music was abandoned and silence restored. Then, just as quickly, it was overthrown.

The doorbell buzzed. In the kitchen, Esther stood motionless, feeling the hoof-kick of nerves. A few seconds passed. The doorbell called again.

'Right, here we go, I suppose,' she said to a photograph of Michael on the windowsill. That funny chin angled left, broad-shouldered in a blue denim shirt, the top two buttons undone. His big face was captured in a moment of serenity, grey eyes trained on something beyond the sights of the camera. Esther imagined what he would say to her and then his voice was in her ears, summoned from a library of memories, talking as if through a seashell. He made a few comments, all practical. His words were encouraging so she stayed there, listening. *I miss you*, Esther said to Michael. He whispered something, a hand on her cheek. Then the doorbell issued its instructions with new ferocity. Michael clicked off. Esther went to let Mr Chartwell in.

The first thing she noticed was that Mr Chartwell was a colossal man. He filled the porch with the silhouette of a mattress, darkening the pane of frosted glass. As she walked towards the front door a weird odour developed and intensified, emanating from the doorway. It smelt like an ancient thing that had been kept permanently damp; a smell of cave soil.

Esther's instincts transmitted high-frequency pulses of intuitive information. They told her that someone odd and kinky awaited her, someone with a rare kinkiness that rode off the spectrum. They told her to hide. But hide where? There was nothing in the hallway to dive behind, it was a wasteland. And what about their appointment? Her dutiful feet pushed forwards.

Opening the door was as violently traumatic as anything could conceivably be, the shock of it blasting out like a klaxon. Esther mashed herself against the wall. She watched with billboard eyes and didn't move.

Mr Chartwell's black lips carved a cordial smile. 'Mrs Esther Hammerhans?' He extended a paw the size of a turnip. 'Hello, I've come about the room.'

3

His fur brushing against her arm as he moved past, Mr Chartwell went down the hall into the kitchen and stood with his ears pricked attentively. He waited there alone. Esther had stayed uselessly by the front door. This was a textbook response, expected. He listened. The noise of a small footstep. Good, she was edging towards the kitchen after him. Here she came, but taking for ever. A headache of adrenalin would blossom as she crept nearer, and, yes, now he could smell it.

Esther stared from the doorway with a blank face as Mr Chartwell poured a cup of stewed black tea. His tongue fell into it and made quiet and industrious progress. He placed the empty cup back on the table and gazed out of the window, mild and horse-like, pretending to admire the view. It was his polite way of giving Esther time to come to terms with the situation. He knew it wasn't easy. Then he turned to face the landlady with an expression that said: I know what you're thinking, but what do you say we just ignore it? The expression also said: Hi there!

Seeing his head move, Esther made a jerk, hands raised over her face.

'Nice garden,' said Mr Chartwell. 'Do you grow vegetables?'

Esther looked at him over a network of fingers. Then the fingers slowly lowered. Terrified, she spoke with all the pepper of lettuce. 'I'm sorry . . . I'm sorry, but you –'

Mr Chartwell nodded with disappointment; it disappointed him that they couldn't ignore the situation as he had hoped.

'You're . . .'

More disappointed nodding.

' . . . A dog . . .'

Mr Chartwell's answer didn't sound unfriendly. 'Yes.'

There was a long silent period where nothing happened. 'You're really enormous for a Labrador,' Esther said finally.

'I'm not a Labrador.' Mr Chartwell leant back against the kitchen counter and folded his arms. He seemed fairly relaxed.

'Are you a ghost?' Esther found a chair at the table and blindly fell into it. ' . . . Some sort of ghost?'

Mr Chartwell said, 'It's pretty obvious I'm a dog. We established that two seconds ago.'

Esther didn't know what to say; she didn't think to say anything. Her eyes moved in steady repeating laps from his head to his feet. Reaching his feet, her eyes leapt to his head, and began their journey again.

Mr Chartwell was unmistakably a dog, a mammoth muscular dog about six foot seven high. He would have been shorter standing on all fours, but was balanced comfortably on hind legs, his inverted knees jutting backwards. He did look similar to a Labrador, with the vast barrelled chest and stocky limbs built to move over rough and difficult terrain, but a heavier-set and strikingly hideous Labrador. There was nothing decorative about him: his short black fur was dense and water-resistant, his broad face split by a vulgar mouth. The monstrous grey tongue dangled, droplets of saliva spilling on to the floor.

Esther took this all in slowly, the horror of him mesmerizing. Her fear began to ebb at the sides. The more she looked the more it ebbed. It melted into a passive state of alarm. Mr Chartwell let her look, although it made him uncomfortable. He wiped a white rope of drool from one crêped lip. There was no way of doing this with any decorum.

Eventually Esther could trust herself to speak to the animal again. 'Are you going to attack me?'

'Not much.' Mr Chartwell said this with disdain.

A pause.

Esther whispered at him, 'You've come about the room?'

'I have,' said Mr Chartwell, pleased they were finally on the right subject.

If she didn't cling to the chair with straining knuckles, Esther felt she would drop and explode over the floor like a collapsing pipe of ash. 'You want to rent my *room?*'

Mr Chartwell nodded. 'I'm keen to move into this area.'

'For how long?' Esther said, and then added immediately, 'Why?'

'Not sure; a few days,' answered Mr Chartwell, not telling her why.

Esther said truthfully, 'I'm really looking to rent out the room for longer than that. A few days is a bit inconvenient.'

'It might be longer, maybe a couple of weeks, perhaps a week.' He broke off. He went over her with his eyes. 'We'll see how it goes,' he said quietly. 'But regardless –' his voice was loud and persuasive now – 'I am able to offer you a unique short-term deal which will make it very convenient.'

There was another pause. Esther looked at him. This was a ridiculous thing to say: nothing could make it convenient.

Mr Chartwell continued. 'For the duration of my residence, Mrs Hammerhans, as recognition of the inconvenience of such a short rental, I can offer you a bulk payment.'

She asked how much. She had to. He was waiting for it.

Mr Chartwell picked from a jackpot. The charismatic chat show host, he said, 'One thousand pounds.' Was it too high? But too late now.

The shock crawled over her face. One thousand pounds was a massive sum, a staggering amount. Esther's annual salary as a library clerk at Westminster Palace was only five hundred pounds. The beast knew the power of his deal, nodding with half-closed, confident eyes, watching her wrestle through the financial possibilities.

But then came a spike of doubt. Where was this money?

'Have you got it with you?' Esther asked. It seemed unlikely. It seemed suspicious.

He repeated quickly, a paw directed at her, directing her to be ambitious, '*One thousand pounds!*'

Esther's eyes pinned him, wanting to ask how a dog could come by that much money. She said nothing for fear of menacing their fragile peace. 'Sorry, are you sure? It's just that it –'

He interrupted. 'I'm sure. One thousand pounds, yes.' He canted forwards, his whiskers in high definition. Another few inches forward. Esther didn't argue.

He spoke again. 'Well, that's the offer. So could we see the room?'

Esther frowned, thinking about this. He wanted to see the room? Let him. What could she actually do to stop him? If he came at her she would be powerless to fight him back. Pitched against him in a struggle, she would be like a sponge thrown against the teeth of a chainsaw. She gestured for him to follow her up the stairs.

Opening the door to the boxroom, Esther's head jolted and met the wall as he went past her, assaulted by the stench of cave soil. Mr Chartwell threw back the crocheted blanket and sheets, testing the mattress underneath with firm jabs. It was found to be satisfactory. The wardrobe door was pumped open and shut several times to check the action. His head disappeared inside to assess the storage space.

Esther said, 'Well, this is it. This is the room.'

Mr Chartwell's eyes were busy. They rested on the rosewood desk against one wall, the wooden chair placed beneath it. The chair held a ruined cushion lined with creases, the filling worn thin. Efforts to whack it into a regular shape were hopeless but it would never be thrown away. The desk carried a regiment of pots full of pencils, pens and trivial antiques. In one pot an ancient stick of rock, in another a plastic toy cow and a drumstick painted with a face. There was a peeled twig among the pencils, a compass and a little ivory carving next to it. Stained rings on the wood showed a history of hot drinks. The desk was a museum. Mr Chartwell's paws went to a drawer and twisted the handle. The handle was loose and he rattled it fondly. He stopped himself.

On the wall above the desk was the small pale square of a removed photograph. Mr Chartwell continued to stare at this pale patch as Esther spoke.

'This room used to be a study. That's why the desk is here.'

Mr Chartwell turned from the absent photograph, fidgeting with his dewlap while he considered everything. He said after a time, 'What about use of the car? Would I have occasional access?'

'No,' Esther lied firmly. 'The lodger would have absolutely no use of the car.'

He looked at her, knowing she was lying. The dewlap was pulled this way and that. His eyes roved across the ceiling. 'And the neighbours, what are they like?'

'Okay, I guess,' said Esther. 'I don't really see them much.' Then, as an afterthought, 'They do have a cat though, so I don't know if that would be a problem –'

Mr Chartwell gave her a sarcastic look. 'Is the cat a problem for you?'

'No,' said Esther. 'I just thought that –' She didn't bother to tell him what she'd thought.

'And there are other lodgers staying here?' said Mr Chartwell.

'No, you'd be the only one,' said Esther.

'I'd be the only one?' Mr Chartwell said, full of hope, assuming this was an invitation.

Esther quickly corrected herself. 'There'd only be one lodger, I mean.'

'And that would be me?' said Mr Chartwell.

'Umm . . .'

A nauseating silent period passed.

Esther said, with exaggerated diplomacy, 'Mr Chartwell, I don't mean to imply that I'm not interested in your offer, or that I think you wouldn't make a very considerate tenant, but I'm not convinced this is going to work out. I was really looking for someone who's more – well, a bit more –'

'You don't like dogs, Mrs Hammerhans?' asked Mr Chartwell.

'No,' Esther answered, 'I do like dogs. Dogs are fine. I'm just not used to them as lodgers. I'm more familiar with them –' and it came out before she could stop it – 'on a pet basis.'

'I'm not a pet,' Mr Chartwell told her.

'I can see that.'

Mr Chartwell's vacant expression suggested he still didn't follow, so she tried to explain. 'I'm thinking primarily about our relationship, about the aspects of that relationship. Say for example you were going to take the room . . .' The delivery of the next line wasn't easy. 'What about if someone gets hurt?'

'Wait, who's getting hurt?' said Mr Chartwell.

Nearly impossible to say: 'Someone who has been mauled.'

Mr Chartwell's voice hit an unpleasant note. 'And why do you suppose anyone would get mauled?'

' . . . Because perhaps –'

Mr Chartwell sighed like an old man, sick of the game. 'Our relationship would be the same as any other landlady and tenant, in so far as I rent the room which you provide. Our responsibilities to each other are strictly limited to this professional understanding. Other than this we won't have anything to do with each other's lives.'

'Right,' Esther said, ashamed, 'right, of course.' She changed the subject. 'Have you lodged anywhere before?'

'Lots of times,' replied Mr Chartwell. 'I have to for work.'

'You work?' said Esther, overwhelmed at the thought. 'What do you do?'

Mr Chartwell ignored her question. 'I do have to reside in this area sporadically, otherwise the commute is a bitch.' He started a comradely conversation about the horrors of a long commute. Esther was still hypnotized by the notion of him working. She asked, 'Your job is here?'

'Sometimes . . . sometimes it is. But it varies. I'm freelance, so I have to travel around to visit my clients.'

'Your clients?' Esther said, curiosity growing in flames.

Mr Chartwell breezed over this. 'So what's your decision about the room?'

Esther pressed her lips together as if rubbing in balm. She didn't have a decision. The morning sun was already strong enough for sunglasses. The trees in the garden grouped against a holiday blue sky. The calling of birds rang out. It was going to be a nice afternoon to sit with a gin and tonic. Esther thought about gin, the bottle in the cupboard singing like a mermaid.

Mr Chartwell saw she was deliberating. He wasn't the deliberating type, preferring action. 'Okay, Mrs Hammerhans, listen, what about if you think it over? You'll probably want to talk it through with your husband.' The sentence was gas, hanging in the air and poisonous.

Esther felt a wave of emotion and recovered herself. 'My husband isn't here at the moment. It'll be my decision.'

'When will he be back?'

Never, Esther thought. 'Later,' she said.

'Right,' Mr Chartwell said. A spark in his face caught her.

'He'll be back later,' Esther said again, watching to see if he believed it.

Mr Chartwell studied her in the same way he had when she had told him about the car, his ugly eyes unrelenting and deliberate. There was a sharp desire to ask what he knew about the situation; he seemed to know something. But what could he know? Instead she said, 'I have to go to work now, so . . . We've got a lot on. A large deadline is approaching and everyone is . . .' She stopped talking about her job; it wouldn't matter to a dog.

'Ah well,' Mr Chartwell said, 'I've got to go to work too.'

What do you *do*? Esther thought, blazing with curiosity.

Mr Chartwell spoke: 'Do you have any plans tonight?'

'Why?'

'Because I could pop round this evening. We can talk about it again.'

'I've got plans.' She didn't.

He said callously, 'You've actually got plans?'

'No.' Esther said it stiffly. 'But I might organize –'

Mr Chartwell didn't wait to hear the rest. 'Fine, then. See you this evening.'

'Oh. Umm . . .' She was defeated, unable to find the courage to argue. 'Okay, but this is not a promise of any kind.' She said in a pathetic voice, 'Don't get your hopes up.'

'Definitely won't,' said Mr Chartwell.

Back at the front door there was an uncomfortable pause. Mr Chartwell put out a paw. Esther's reluctant hand held the paw as if clasping a grenade. They engaged in a weird handshake.

'So –' she said, Mr Chartwell speaking at the same time. They did the dance of halting awkwardness, the normal chemistry of conversation wildly absent. 'Right,' said Mr Chartwell, and Esther said, 'Oka–'

'Right,' he said again.

Then Mr Chartwell shook his head vigorously, the ruff round his neck slinging about, a good wet noise coming from his loose cheeks as they slapped against his gums. 'Well, goodbye,' he said, and closed the door behind him. Esther listened to him thump down on to four feet, the sound of claws on concrete, and then the heavy, meaty sound of a powerful animal tanking forward with determination.

4

Churchill was outside near the lake in the lower grounds. Standing above on the tiered garden slopes, the house watched. A tall, lonely lookout, its red bricks were stark against the darkness of the ivy-webbed forest which pushed hard against it. The tranquillity of Churchill's lawns and gardens belied the enduring battle against the medieval forest's attempts to reclaim them. Growing from a brown carpet of leaves cross-hatched with animal tracks, an army of trunks and branches advanced together. Fallen oaks and pines exposed huge plates of knotted roots covered in rust red earth, juvenile troops sending out shoots the colour of celery.

Churchill was at the lake to paint a picture of the scenery, a task that required he wear his shapeless artist's smock and a sombrero. A selection of battered paintbrushes and jars, pencils and paints lay on the grass around him. He preferred to stand when he painted; it gave him a freedom of movement that sitting didn't allow. Not that this freedom meant anything, because he was standing motionless in front of the easel, arms hanging at his sides. The small canvas balanced on the easel was untouched.

He muttered a phrase he had often repeated: 'Happy are the painters, for they shall not be lonely.' This seemed absurd to him now, as he did not feel it.

Churchill frowned, his lower jaw thrust over his collar. From the sombrero's shadow his eyes followed a pair of black swans circling in the water. They had come over to him, expecting bread, necks high, but finding none had drifted off. A coot let out a sharp shriek from the bulrushes. A gust of wind moved an old Scots pine nearby, shaking its needles and losing a few infant cones. Ripples moved across the lake, distorting the reflection of the cloudless sky. Churchill's companion, a brown poodle named Rufus, had long since disappeared, heading off to the orchards where the servants' cottages were, spooked and unwilling to stay at his side. Churchill knew what worried him. And then there it was.

Behind him it whispered ardently in his ear, 'You can't hide from me. And you look ridiculous in that smock. You look like an old toad.'

Churchill didn't answer.

'Ribbit,' said the voice. It broke away to snigger madly to itself, then returned. '*Ribbit,*' it said with perverse menace.

The swans blurred as Churchill's eyes misted. This was an involuntary reaction, an unwelcome one. He put his left thumb in the palm and crushed it.

'You've been expecting me,' said the heartless voice. 'You've been waiting for me, I could hear you waiting.'

Churchill thought of his meeting that afternoon, willing the time to fold, wishing to escape the gruelling static of the hours in between. He thought of the meeting and clung to it, trying to block out the voice.

It spoke again, quieter and closer now, close enough for him to feel that warm, carnivorous breath. 'We both know why I'm here.'

'Bugger off, you tiresome bastard,' Churchill said viciously.

The hot breath blew across his cheek, across his neck. '*We have an appointment.*'

5

Esther hid behind a partition of books in room B, a high, wooden reading room in the House of Commons library. Around her the shelves were filled with many thousands of books. In the centre of one wall was a wide stone fireplace with an ornamental fireguard. The London outside was white, pale blue and boisterous. Not here. Room B was sombre and chaste, a scholarly cathedral of dark wood, richly patterned carpet and green leather. Discreet ladders leant in places, the oak glossed with years of use. A heroic climb took the library clerks to the top-roosting books, then a worse one-handed climb down. Understated chandeliers with glass shades were suspended from brass chains. Two lead-latticed windows at the far end of the room gazed out on a Thames lit cardboard-brown in the sun.

The library was laid out like a gallery in a Tudor house. A long corridor ran through the centre of each room. Behind Esther an arched wooden doorway led to other, more peopled areas of the library – the reading rooms C and D, the reference and oriel room, room A ahead. Sounds of life drifted towards her.

That deserted haven, room B. Esther was hunched over her desk, the surface stacked with books, needing to concentrate. Thoughts of Mr Chartwell and his visit were a wound which wanted its bandages quietly lifted to assess, stomach in flight, what lay underneath. An abomination, an abominable thing. Esther sat there dissecting the details.

The noise of Beth Oliver shoving some books aside with her heavy hip as she sat on the desk startled Esther.

Beth's face was attractive and comfortable, with a smile full of natural sugars. She had a relaxed sensuality which expressed itself in an appetite for everything, including the carrot she was now admiring between bites. Trapping her wavy bobbed hair behind an ear made no difference, the hair breaking free. Using the tip of the carrot to push it ended in hair stuck to the carrot.

'Hi, Esther, what are you doing?'

'Oh, nothing much, just my job or something,' Esther said in the sterile voice she used when she didn't want to talk.

'Ha, yeah,' said Beth, flicking distractedly through a book on top of the pile. It was entitled *Roman Architecture in the West Midlands of England*. She let the pages run over her fingers. 'So come on. Tell me.'

Bumping herself further on to the table caused a column of books to slide on to Esther's lap. Esther caught the avalanche without comment and heaped it back. 'Tell you what?'

'Tell me all about the incarnation of your tiny boxy study into a luxury bedroom. That's why I gave you that horrible old bed, isn't it? So you could rent it to some unsuspecting victim.'

'The bed's not so bad with some new sheets on it.' Esther smiled at her. 'As long as you don't sit on it or lie on it, it looks quite nice.'

'It looks quite nice? Those must be some miraculous sheets. Didn't you say someone came to look at the room this morning?'

Esther picked up a pen and toyed with it. 'Someone did.'

'Exciting! And when is this unlucky lodger moving in?'

The pen lid was chewed and came away in her mouth. Esther spoke with the lid between her teeth. 'Oh, I don't know.' 'I'm not sure yet.'

But Beth had been distracted, grinning and doing something with her hands. Esther bent to see, leaning in her chair. The legs lifted as she craned round the doorway. It was the Head of the Library, John Dennis-John, hammering a typewriter in his characteristic warrior way at a desk in reception. Beth mimicked him, pretending to type with punching fists on a book. Dennis-John looked up with a snap, his instincts sonic. Esther ducked, her chair thumping down. Caught in his crossfire, Beth made an act of straightening her skirt. A good act, Esther thought, as she watched Beth fight off a smile.

A snort of laughter from Esther, a match-flare of amusement which died instantly.

Beth made a quick check on Dennis-John, stretching her neck. She waited for his typing to resume. She turned and studied Esther.

'Es?' Beth locked an elbow, watching her. 'Are you all right?'

'I'm fine, yep. Just a bit tired.' It wasn't convincing.

Beth's posture developed a sarcastic accent. 'Don't tell me that, it won't wash because I know you too well, Hammerhans. I know when you're hiding something from me.'

'I'm really busy, that's all.'

'Busy with what?' Beth tossed the books about, hunting for a theme. 'With this?' The area outside suddenly bustled with bodies, a group of library clerks chattering as they entered from the three-mile maze of corridors in Westminster Palace. The gentle swell of conversation was punctuated by a shot of laughter, the plastic note of Sellotape being stretched and torn from its holder. A phone rang and was answered. Beth's thumb tapped across the books and chose one for inspection. She lifted it by the cover, the pages hanging. '*Saints of Ireland, England, Scotland and Wales* . . . what is this, Esther?'

'I've got to type up some notes for the Prime Minister,' Esther lied, making notes, printing tiny letters in a notebook. 'He needs me to do some research.'

'Notes for Douglas-Home on saints? A very likely story.' Beth let the book fall. 'Nope,' she said, 'I think I recognize that secret look.

Ah yes, I know what's going on here . . . Esther, have you met someone?'

Esther clucked her tongue.

'Have you been on a date?' Beth said this with joyous hope, excited by her own imagination, seeing Esther in a restaurant, candles and two spoons with dessert.

'Nothing like that, unfortunately,' answered Esther. 'It's quite hard to explain exactly how unlike that . . .'

'Ladies and gentlemen of the *jury*,' Beth said with saucy solemnity, addressing an invisible crowd, 'I present you with our coy exhibit, a dear friend who stands in contempt of the court if she fails to indulge the judge with every detail of her date.'

'Stop it, there is no date.' Her voice was unintentionally cold.

Puzzled at the reaction, Beth pulled away. A quality in Esther echoed, too faint to decipher. What? No, it faded, Beth mistaken.

'I'm only playing around, Es.'

Esther spoke to the notebook. 'I don't want to play.'

Beth started a friendly argument and was stopped. 'There is no date and I don't want to play, Beth. Let's just change the subject.'

'Okay . . .' Beth rolled her chin in apology. 'I'm sorry. For a second I thought you might have.' A hand lifted in a justifying flip, landing flat against the table. 'Well, it's not so ridiculous, is it? You're not *too* hideous, Es.'

Down among the books Esther didn't respond, carrying on with her notes. A quick and horrible feeling in the guts acknowledged that she was being unfair to Beth. And her mood couldn't entirely be blamed on Mr Chartwell. There was another reason, a darker, emptier one that ate through the calendar countdown of four days. Esther chastised herself for feeling disappointed that Beth hadn't remembered, knowing she would soon. And she knew with a complicated knot in her chest that she would almost rather Beth didn't.

Beth curved her mouth, the sad bulldog, trying for a laugh and failing. 'I'm only joking.' Esther's attitude was a mystery. She spoke to the top of Esther's head. 'Come on, Es, I'm only joking. Don't get in a twist.'

Esther blew up her fringe. 'It's not funny, Beth. You know how I feel.'

'*Ksssss.*' Beth made a noise in air between her teeth. 'I know, I know, I know.'

'Well then,' said Esther. She dropped the volume as a tall man and a woman walked into room B, the woman's high heels ticking across the floor. The man followed awkwardly. 'Don't joke about it.'

Beth's eyes nipped to monitor the couple. 'I'm sorry. It's just that . . .' She willed the clerks away. ' . . . It's just that it was such a long time ago. Michael was such a long time ago. I suppose I . . .' She reached over and moved Esther's fringe to one side, styling it. Esther had a grace which made her striking, with a face whose beauty came in subtle ways. 'You're a pretty girl, Es. We only want you to be happy.'

Beth was impossible to ignore. 'We love you, you know. I do, me and Big Oliver love you.' Big Oliver was Beth's husband, a kind and solid man.

Esther looked at her. For countless hours, an arm round her shoulders, Beth had listened. And remembering this, Esther's heart burst like an egg yolk. Her hands opened in surrender: Trust me, Beth, I annoy myself.

Seeing she was forgiven, Beth immediately pushed Esther's nose up with a finger. 'Darling Es, we just want you to meet another nice man and fall in love and have lots of little piglets.'

Esther pushed Beth's finger away. 'I'm not ready yet. Maybe in a little while I'll be able to –'

But being forgiven, Beth cut her off, catching her with an elbow. 'In a little while? Tchk. I've heard that one before.'

She fetched a lipstick from a pocket and applied it flawlessly.

Snatching Esther's notebook, she carefully blotted her lips on the page and presented it to her.

'Beth!' Esther looked at the red mouth across her notes.

Over at the window the library clerk was pointing out Lambeth Palace to the man. He asked some questions to the back of her blouse and she rotated to indicate with air-hostess arms at a row of shelves. A friendly grin abandoned him at the window. He stared after her with restrained apprehension. He consulted the thick orienteering booklet given to new members of staff. The sound of ransacked paper became faster and ended as he flipped to read the index.

Esther was still staring at Beth's paper kiss.

'Bup, bup, bup!' said Beth as Esther began to complain, a finger in the air. 'Now there's your –'

She was interrupted, the man appearing next to them. 'Ah, hello.' He touched the knot of his tie. 'Hello, I wonder if you could help me.'

'This is your first day here?' asked Beth. It was and she whistled. 'Good luck, you'll need it.' Outrageous, as it was only a library. 'And let me guess, you want to find the loos.'

He knocked his eyes to the side. 'Um . . . yes.'

Beth told him, drawing a map in the air with helpful landmarks.

'Right,' said the man. 'Right, thanks.'

'I could show you, if that's easier,' said Esther.

He smiled at her, liking her soft, sleepy-toned voice. 'No, I'll probably manage. Thank you though.'

He started to leave, then turned at the doorway. 'My name's Mark Corkbowl, by the way.' He added as a useless explanation, 'Just, ah . . . just so you know my name.'

'Good to meet you, Corkbowl,' answered Beth.

'You can call me Mark if you . . .'

Beth didn't hear him. 'Come and find me if you need anything, Corkbowl.'

'Or call me Corkbowl,' he said quietly. 'Corkbowl is fine.' He gave them a wave, trying to be the casual man. He walked off, magnificently anti-casual.

Beth grinned at his retreating figure before reaching over to give the notebook a few rapping taps. 'There's your first kiss for free, Es. Now you have to start collecting others, otherwise your membership will expire.'

'Will do, Beth.' Esther tore off the page, putting it to one side. 'I just need to meet someone who makes me want to be a member.'

Beth slipped from the desk, giving Esther a chipper wink as she left. 'Michael would want you to find someone and kiss them. If he was here he would order you to immediately.'

If he was here, thought Esther as she balled Beth's kiss and threw it in the bin, if he was bloody here then I wouldn't need to.

6

'Before we start, thank you all for coming today,' said the Prime Minister. 'It's a busy Wednesday afternoon and I don't want to keep you long.'

A chorus of agreement was followed by the sound of everyone around the large U-shaped table sipping coffee simultaneously. They were gathered in one of the committee rooms that ran off Committee Corridor, situated roughly above the Commons library and sharing a view of the Thames. With wood panelling and Pugin wallpaper, the room was elaborate and stately.

After a suitable pause Sir Alec Douglas-Home said, 'As you know, we are here to discuss briefly the resignation from parliament of our much tried and never bettered colleague, Member for Woodford, and Father of the House, Sir Winston Churchill.'

All eyes turned to Churchill, who sat at one end of the table wearing a single-breasted grey wool suit. He removed his cigar in a salute. It was a Romeo y Julieta, the favourite brand regularly found clamped between his teeth, lit or not. This one was lit; grey vines of smoke climbed to the ceiling.

Douglas-Home continued. 'Sir Winston will be leaving the House of Commons for the final time on the twenty-seventh of July, after a political career which has spanned sixty years.'

'Sixty-four years,' said Churchill.

Douglas-Home nodded at this correction. 'And the following day I will be heading a deputation of parliamentary members, including Harold Wilson and Jo Grimond, to present Sir Winston with a

Resolution to mark his forthcoming retirement and express our gratitude for his outstanding services. The press have been informed and will be covering this event. And naturally, on the twenty-seventh we expect a very large public gathering to see the great man off . . .'

Receiving a stinging glare from Churchill, he amended his tone. 'It will be a sad day for Britain when you go, Winston; a sad day and a historic day, ending a truly historic era in our government, one which we shall always remember.' He added, 'I am privileged to have some personal memories of this era myself, as our paths have been somewhat entwined. I particularly value my time during your second term as Prime Minister when I served as Minister of State at the Scottish Office.'

'Ah yes,' the chewed cigar came out, 'back when I was still a spring chicken on the cusp of seventy-seven.'

'You may have been seventy-seven in age, but never,' Douglas-Home said with a smile, 'as I recall, much in manner. I have to admit I do sometimes wonder where you found your vitality.' He joked, 'And I say this as both a sprightly sixty-one-year-old and, as I always like to remind everyone, the only Prime Minister to have played first-class cricket.' Douglas-Home was a genial man, with fine features and an easy humour.

'Thank you, Alec,' Churchill answered. 'Yes, that's praise indeed, especially coming from such an accomplished young sportsman.'

Douglas-Home laughed at this, then said with warm respect, 'What you have achieved in your life is truly remarkable, Winston. As you yourself have said, you felt as though you were walking with destiny. And there is no doubt you fulfilled your destiny. Yours has been a role of crucial importance, one I doubt any other man could have faced with the same resolution and tenacity.'

With this rousing speech, a feeling of high emotion coursed beneath the dark suits of the politicians. They hid it for the most part, but couldn't refrain from studying the robust figure in front of them. Their eyes sought to remember each detail and store it.

Churchill's Turnbull & Asser bow tie, a distinctive spotted model as always, was bothering him as he acknowledged the men. He repressed the urge to tear it from his neck and hurl it across the room. He was not enjoying being there; while leaving parliament was a difficult thing to think about, the prospect of retirement could not yet be fully contemplated, being too full of awful passion. It churned the heart with thistles. Another bad night's sleep hadn't helped, exacerbated by the episode at the lake, and it left him feeling immobile and annoyed. He longed to go back to his home, to Chartwell, and relax in the hospital of his bed with a brandy.

There was a shuffling of papers as the meeting drew to an end.

'So,' said Douglas-Home, 'now we are all clear on the subject I propose that we get back to business. Thank you, gentlemen.'

Churchill rose stiffly from his chair, the cigar dead in his mouth. Putting on his black Bowker hat and throwing his coat over one arm, he stumped through the Victorian gothic labyrinth of Westminster Palace, heels ringing on the ornate Minton tiles of the corridors, to the car waiting outside. The cigar was fired up again in the back seat, the carriage filling with pale, curling waves. Churchill stared solemnly through the window as the driver pulled away from the kerb. 'K.B.O., K.B.O.,' he said to no one.

'Sorry, what was that, sir?' asked the driver.

Churchill smiled. 'Nothing, old chap, nothing. Just a phrase I use as sustenance in problematical times.'

'K.B.O.?' The driver cast a look at him in the rear-view mirror. 'Is that a political acronym?'

'Ha, no. Nothing like that. It stands for keep buggering on.'

The driver's eyes returned to the road as they swept round a corner. 'Seems like very sound advice to me, sir.'

Churchill said, 'It's certainly a doctrine I subscribe to, my man. Yes, keep buggering on.'

7

6.00 p.m.

The pavements and buildings of Westminster radiated heat, throwing out the sun absorbed over hours of intensive baking. The grass, dried to its yellow roots, crunched underfoot. A sandstone path took Esther to the iron gate of Black Rod's entrance. It clanged back on its hinges. Walking from the cool of the library on to the streets made the eyes spark with dots. Esther took it slowly as she went to her car. She drank from a glass bottle of hot Fanta and was sickened by it.

Mr Chartwell's imminent appointment loomed like the promise of an accident and was terrible. But extraordinarily, the idea that he wouldn't come, disappearing for ever, was also terrible. These two terrors battled for supremacy. Then, thrashed into submission, one fell beneath the other. Starting the car ignition, Esther was fascinated to discover she secretly wanted Mr Chartwell to come to the house. It made her turn off the engine, needing to sit for a minute and check the facts.

For a long time the weeks of her life had drifted past as ghosts. There was the rare bump of pleasure, perhaps from a meal out or a visit to the cinema, but it was brittle and shattered under the lonely monotony of the ghost days. But now the singular Mr Chartwell was here, ransacking her forlorn routine. It was a tonic of acid vibrancy and nerves.

At home she moved about like an animal running around the walls of its compound, useless with anxiety. It was a relief when there was a knock at the front door which told her the familiar mattress shape would be blocking the light in her hallway.

'Hello, Mrs Hammerhans,' said Mr Chartwell. He was holding a bunch of exhausted carnations, which he handed to her, then stood panting loudly. When Esther offered him a glass of water he reached behind a hind leg, producing a bottle of Mateus Rosé hidden on the doorstep. 'I thought you might like some wine.'

'Oh,' Esther said in surprise, wondering where he'd bought it, 'that sounds nice.' She added as an afterthought, 'Call me Esther. You don't need to call me Mrs Hammerhans.'

In the kitchen he stood clumsy and self-conscious, leaning a paw on the orange tiles over the counter as Esther fetched the glasses. She said, 'What do you think about having a drink in the garden? It's a lovely evening.'

Mr Chartwell murmured his consent and padded tamely behind her, Esther fighting the impulse to squirm off on the legs of an octopus at his closeness.

The garden, a modest strip of land preserved as Michael had left it, had been lovingly bullied into opulence. Swollen in the summer sun and bulging with flowers, it looked like a burst suitcase. Birch trees grew near a pond, big red goldfish breaking the water as they lipped the surface for insects. Mr Chartwell watched them avidly, ears tuned to their activities.

Esther sat down on the bench. She leant back, dust from the kitchen windowsill coating her hair, and drank some wine. It was warm and offensively sweet, a foul syrup, but Esther welcomed it. She topped up her glass.

Mr Chartwell was finished with the fish and went to look at the greenhouse. Hidden in a passageway along one side of the house, it was ripe with tomato plants and courgettes, leaves crowding the glass.

'Nice tomatoes,' said Mr Chartwell.

'Thanks, I grew them myself,' Esther said, as though it would surprise anyone.

'What are you going to do with them?' Mr Chartwell asked.

'I don't know, eat them I suppose,' Esther said.

'Right,' said Mr Chartwell, as if this was big news. 'I've got a great chutney recipe. Perhaps you'd like it?'

Esther didn't like it. She didn't want any recipe recommended by a dog. Terrified of causing offence, she smiled weakly. 'Thank you. That would be good.'

'I've got a fantastic jam recipe, too,' said Mr Chartwell, spotting some strawberry plants and smirking at the joke he was about to make. 'In fact my jam is the last word in fine preserves. I should give you a jar so you can *spread* the word . . .' Turned away from her, his shoulders shook.

Then he came towards the bench.

Esther stiffened. He was going to sit next to her? The idea was horrifying. She bit into her inner cheek, hurting it, and wanted to leap away. She fumbled through a list of excuses, all unusable, and shocked herself by being on the verge of tears.

She needn't have worried. Mr Chartwell put his glass of wine down and dropped on to all fours. In front of the bench a long bald patch was worn through the grass, the soil beneath dried into sand. He made a few turns on this spot, clawing the area, and capsized on to his side, legs stretched out. The grassless trench was perfectly sized.

'Ah, relaxing here on the lawn,' he said with great satisfaction, wagging his tail. It made the sound of a hockey stick thumping the ground. He picked up his wineglass. The fingerless paw had no difficulty gripping the stem, but his coffin mouth and immobile lips made drinking from it awkward. The wine wanted to pour across the sides of his face in streams. After each sip he fought the wine, working his jaws, which produced an indecent smacking sound. Droplets sprayed into the air, some landing on Esther's feet.

They listened to the squabbling of birds.

'Have you given any more thought to what we talked about this morning?' asked Mr Chartwell.

Esther said, 'I've thought about it a lot actually.'

'Have you made your mind up?'

Esther took a slow, hesitant sip of wine. 'I haven't, no.'

'I see,' said Mr Chartwell, in a way which implied that this was a powerfully boring answer. 'Because I do really need to confirm where I'll be staying as quickly as possible.'

'Have you looked anywhere else? At any other houses?' Esther asked.

'A few places, none as convenient as this one.'

Mr Chartwell rolled a paw as he explained. 'The location here is hard to beat in terms of convenience for work. Door to door I'm looking at a fifty-minute journey.' He laid his head on the ground, half his face hidden. The one visible eye swivelled to look at Esther.

She made a thoughtful hum. 'And you say it will only be for a few days? After that you're leaving?'

'Probably.' Mr Chartwell yawned, a high-pitched animal noise leaving his throat.

'Right,' said Esther. A fish caught a beetle with a splash.

She tried to draw more from Mr Chartwell. 'So how many days do you think?'

'Don't know,' Mr Chartwell said.

'And this is for your work?'

'Yup,' he said.

'And you'll pay me one thousand pounds?'

'Yup.'

'Regardless of the time you stay, you'll pay me one thousand pounds?'

'Correct.'

'That certainly is a lot of money . . .'

'Certainly is.' He gave something on the grass an investigatory lick.

Esther said as an invitation, 'Your job must pay you an awful lot . . .'

Mr Chartwell was still busy licking.

Esther waited for him to finish. When he didn't she felt a rising fury at his evasiveness. He was doing it on purpose, refusing to answer her! Well, try and evade this! She leant forward on her knees. 'Mr Chartwell, listen, with all respect I don't know anything about you. Don't you think I should know more about you if you want to move in?'

'Oh, you want to know more about me?' Mr Chartwell said, tongue out. 'Okay, I don't like beetroot.'

'Right,' Esther answered with slight bite. 'And what about the rest? What about absolutely everything else? . . . You haven't told me what you do for a living, what your first name is, what you're doing here, or anything. I don't even know what you are. I think you owe me some sort of an explanation.'

Mr Chartwell arranged his face to display the highest level of scorn. 'You think your position of landlady necessitates that I tell you every-thing about my circumstances?'

Made nervous by his attack, Esther said, 'I don't think it's so awful to ask you. I think anyone would be –'

'Well, can I expect you to tell me about yourself in return?' Mr Chartwell interrupted.

'Why?'

He watched her face.

Esther shrugged. 'I guess so.'

' . . . You'll talk honestly about your life?'

'It's no secret,' she said, although it was.

While Mr Chartwell considered this, his whiskery eyebrows moved. They weren't eyebrows as much as thumbprint-sized buds above his eyes, but they were expressive in the same way. A ladybird landed on his thigh and the leg kicked out in an impulsive move.

'Fine,' he said eventually. 'I don't usually do this, but I can make a concession on this occasion, under the strict understanding that this information is absolutely confidential.'

'Absolutely,' said Esther. She felt Mr Chartwell studying her again and didn't meet his eyes, making an ordeal of examining her wine, dipping a finger to retrieve an imaginary fly, then checking the glass again from all angles.

With a grunt Mr Chartwell heaved himself up. He didn't rise on to his two back legs this time, choosing to walk informally on all fours. Although he moved easily on two legs it looked oafish, as if invisible hands were lifting him under the arms. It reminded Esther of a child holding up a cat to make it dance with its hind paws.

She followed behind. 'Don't you want to stay outside? It's still warm.'

Mr Chartwell gave her a shot of his profile. 'I can't risk being overheard.' He reached up, turned the door handle and then pushed through, filling the doorway.

8

Mr Chartwell wedged himself into a wooden chair at the powder blue Formica-topped table. The chair sent out a ripple of creaks at his weight. The yellow kitchen wall behind him was a complementary backdrop for his jet black fur. Opposite him, Esther sat with the incredible posture of the very edgy. The promise of revelation had created a sense of electricity in the room. But while the tension made Esther worry, Mr Chartwell was quiet with deep monastic contemplation.

Not wanting to be distracted by hunger, she had laid out a plate with some cheeses and a handful of crackers. They lay unmolested. The weight of expectation building, it became a contest to see who could remain silent the longest. Esther trapped a sound against the roof of her mouth before it became a recognizable word. Then Mr Chartwell cleared his throat. Esther leant forward.

'Could I have some of the Red Leicester?' he asked, carving a great chunk of it off with the knife. He shovelled it in and resumed his thinking. They both listened to him chew. Not just a sickening noise, it was also a vigorous one. The shape of his face didn't permit quiet eating, or subtle eating with a closed mouth. Loud and visible, the cheese mashed into a pulp.

The Red Leicester finished, Mr Chartwell went to speak again. 'And that Cheshire, do you mind?' Another slab was hacked off and fed through the jaws. Crumbs fell from his teeth, littering the table and the fur on his chest. He wiped at the crumbs and this made it worse.

Esther couldn't look at him. To distract herself she started humming 'Do Wah Diddy Diddy' by Manfred Mann. Unable to concentrate, the hummed tune developed an abnormal pitch. It was razor wire to Mr Chartwell's acutely sensitive ears. He relented at last with an enormous sigh.

'Look, as I said in the garden, I'm really not happy about having to do this. The only reason I'm agreeing to tell you anything is because I believe it when you say you won't tell anyone. You seem like a private person.'

Esther nodded sincerely. 'Really private. I won't tell anyone.'

'Excellent.' Gathering his thoughts, Mr Chartwell put his paws to his temples and pulled slightly. This stretched his cheeks back, revealing teeth that would not normally be seen. His eyelids also pulled, showing their rims.

Esther watched this behaviour sceptically.

'So then, let's start with what you do?' she asked. There followed another frustrating silence. Refusing to participate, Esther surveyed the room. She studied the antique dresser pushed against one wall. It was loaded with worthless but friendly trinkets collected over the years: photographs and fraying postcards, painted plates, a pair of novelty Punch and Judy eggcups, a metal jelly mould. They had been selected carefully. The dresser was more than a storage place for holiday trophies; it was a strategic device for forcing good memories to the lid of the mind, a raft in a sea of empty grief. Over the twin blockade of a china lighthouse and a wooden elephant, Michael's forehead creased at her. His early-greying hair, with all the style of a tuft of old wool, flew up to meet the breeze. Obscured from view in the photograph, Esther was folded in his arms, one eye closed, her mouth captured grousing about the rain. They had been on a beach in Cornwall.

'What do *you* do?' Mr Chartwell shot back, ending the stand-off.

Esther looked at him. 'I work in Westminster Palace as a library clerk. I've worked there for six years now. It's okay.' Esther smiled in the way that said: hey ho. She said, knowing it was foolish, 'I don't suppose you do anything similar?'

Mr Chartwell shook his head, entertained by this. 'No, nothing similar at all. I'm a specialist. I provide specific services for varying lengths of time to specific individuals.'

'What services?' asked Esther.

Mr Chartwell exhaled. He took another breath, exhaled again.

'It might be easier to start by discussing my current client. That might make it easier to understand.'

Esther prepared herself. 'Who's your client, then?'

'A political great,' answered Mr Chartwell.

'Abraham Lincoln?' said Esther.

'A British political great.'

'Oliver Cromwell.'

'A living British political great,' Mr Chartwell said patiently.

Esther thought for a minute. 'Winston Churchill?'

Mr Chartwell nodded in a sweeping movement. 'Yup.'

Surely a hoax, she waited for him to confess. Not a hoax, he looked at her with expressionless sincerity. So it was true. The impossibility of the idea, its hysterical strangeness, made Esther slump against her chair. 'You work with Winston Churchill?'

'I do,' said Mr Chartwell. 'I have done on and off for a long time.'

The clock beat out a few seconds.

'Are you friends?' said Esther.

Mr Chartwell answered quickly and decidedly. 'Oh no, oho no, we most certainly are not, although we know each other very well.'

Esther leant in and looked into Mr Chartwell's face, trying to divine the truth. 'You don't like each other?'

Using the knife skilfully, Mr Chartwell sliced a hoggish chunk of Cheddar. He threw it into his mouth, teeth snapping together like a trap. 'Actually I do rather like him. But he fears and despises me.' Mr Chartwell shrugged in a way that suggested he was used to it.

Esther said in a papery voice, 'Why?'

'Because the service I provide is not much fun.'

Esther waited before allowing herself to say anything else. 'What's the service?'

Mr Chartwell's eyes moved around the room. He started to say something and then stopped. 'I'm finding it quite difficult to talk about,' he said at last.

'Is it really awful?' asked Esther, scared. 'Do you hurt people?'

'Not as such,' Mr Chartwell said slowly. 'I don't actually hurt them.' He searched for the words, a paw circling.

Esther spoke. 'Yes you do, I bet you do.'

'No,' Mr Chartwell said testily. 'I depress them.'

Esther was still. 'You depress them? As in you crush them? As in by depress you mean weight?'

Mr Chartwell made an explanatory gesture. 'The weight is emotional, if you want to use those basic terms –' a little twitch in his face showed he reserved a less flattering opinion of the terms – 'so indirectly, perhaps.'

'Emotional weight? I don't . . .' Esther unconsciously reached for a cracker. The cracker was extremely dry. The room was silent apart from the sound of her grinding it to dust. 'What do you mean?'

'Exactly that. My services consist of periods of time when I visit specific people, people who experience a specific darkness. Churchill is a regular.' Mr Chartwell made this next disclosure carefully. 'He names his depression the Black Dog.'

A choke was overpowered. 'You are the Black Dog?'

'Obviously,' said Mr Chartwell.

'Haven't you told him your name is Mr Chartwell?'

'That's not really my name. I made it up for your benefit.'

Esther started as she realized something. 'Chartwell is the name of Churchill's house, isn't it?'

'It is,' confirmed Mr Chartwell.

'Do you call yourself the Black Dog?'

He moved his brow. 'No, it's not much of a name, is it? Really more of a description, although I don't mind it.'

'It's pretty accurate,' said Esther. 'It is what you are.'

He smiled: he was undeniably a black dog.

'So what's your real name?' Esther asked.

Mr Chartwell puffed some air out between his lips. It made an unpleasant vibrating sound. He reached an arm up, letting it rest across his head. 'My real name? Phew . . . okay, my real name is . . .' He paused, frowning in concentration, one paw meddling with an ear. 'My real name is Black Patrick.'

It was a definite lie. Esther said, 'That's not your name.'

'No, but it's a name I like. I certainly like it more than the Black Dog.' He tested out Black Patrick and then the shortened Black Pat a few times to himself before saying, 'You can call me Black Pat.'

'What's your actual name?'

'I think we'll stick with Black Pat Chartwell for now,' Mr Chartwell said firmly. It was clear that the discussion was finished. 'Call me Black Pat.'

A frightening thought occurred to Esther. 'Wait, what would happen if Churchill knew you were here? What if he knew I was talking about letting you stay here? If I let you stay here to depress him, I'd be profiting from his misery.'

'Don't worry about it,' said Black Pat. 'He's too depressed to do anything but loaf around watching his black swans.'

'But it seems immoral for me to help in assisting with this. It feels so deeply immoral. Mr Chartwell, I can't be a part of it.'

Black Pat Chartwell sprawled across the table. 'First of all, *Esther*, as we just discussed, call me Black Pat. Secondly, my business is none of your concern. It's between me and the client. Thirdly, this is just something that has to happen. It happens to a lot of people. You, Esther, should know this.'

That quality in his tone did not invite questions. Esther watched him with a tight mistrustful mouth, wondering what he meant.

Black Pat didn't speak.

She said, 'It's a very weird situation. Terrible.'

He filled his chest and strained back against the chair, stretching. 'Just a job. I'm just doing my job, that's all.'

'Your job is extremely cruel, Black Pat,' said Esther. She had another thought. 'What do you do all day? How do you make people depressed?'

Black Pat's ears, which usually hung down the sides of his face, lifted to stand higher. It was a sure sign he was engaged with the conversation. 'It's hard to explain. With Churchill we know each other's movements, so we have a routine, I guess. I like to be there when he wakes up in the morning. Sometimes I drape across his chest. That slows him down for a bit. And then I like to lie around in the corner of the room, crying out like I have terrible injuries. Sometimes I'll burst out at him from behind some furniture and bark in his face. During meals I'll squat near his plate and breathe over his food. I might lean on him too when he's standing up, or hang off him in some way. I also make an effort to block out the sunlight whenever I can.' He gave her a sloped glance. 'Ha. Ack, not really. I'm making light of it, trying to make a joke.' He slid his eyes away in a sort of embarrassment. 'I don't like talking about the operational intricacies, it's unsavoury.'

'Whatever it is, it still sounds horrible,' said Esther.

'It certainly gets him down,' agreed Black Pat.

'Do you ever give him a break?'

'Nope. He's wily though, so I have to watch him. He might look depressed, but in fact he'll be concentrating on a book. When I catch him reading I sit next to him and chew rocks. The sound drives him crazy, absolutely crazy.'

'And do you do this for everyone?' asked Esther.

'Everyone has a different way of working, so it changes,' Black Pat answered.

Esther suddenly had an uneasy feeling, a nag of apprehension. She dug a fingernail into the soft plastic rim running around the edge of the table. 'What would happen to me? How would I know?'

Black Pat said immediately, 'You tell me.'

9

8.00 p.m.

The ground floor of the Olivers' home, an impressive detached house in Barnes, was a luxurious showroom for open-plan living.

The living area was on a split level, divided from the dining room. It was populated by low bookcases, sofas and chairs with buttoned upholstery, mostly pale green, and a couple of rya-style rugs. Above one of the armchairs, Big Oliver's specific chair, a standard lamp arched overhead on its metal arm. This was a new addition to the house and still exciting. Next to the lamp was a John Piper print.

The dining area, a fine example of Scandinavian modernism, was dominated along one wall by an expensive model of system furnishing: exotic rosewood units suspended from batons at fashionably diverse levels. The lower units were dressed with two stylish wood and spun aluminium lamps, a marble horse galloping with its mane flung into thick peaks, and a bulbous glass vase with a miniature garden of ferns inside. A small African antelope-skin drum lived on top of the drinks cabinet, the cabinet's sliding door clad with dimpled bronze. The higher units displayed small ethnic sculptures and framed photographs of Beth and her husband Big Oliver, all artistic and flattering. One larger photograph showed Beth holding their son Little Oliver in a tasselled white blanket at his christening, Big Oliver standing with his arm around her. Little Oliver, now three years old, was in bed. Over the dining table a spot lamp complete with counterbalanced mechanism and anodized aluminium shade hung low, shining into the mouth of an empty bottle of tomato sauce.

Leaving the finished dinner plates on the dining table, Beth went barefoot past the open French windows, heading from the dining level to the sofa. Thumping steps came down the stairs, Big Oliver entering with one of Little Oliver's hats on his head, perched there as a joke, a tiny hat on a giant adult head. Just back from checking on their son, he was now smashing around in the kitchen, always loud.

The Clerk of the Parliaments at Westminster, he was a heavily constructed man, with the build of a boxer when younger although he had never tested it. Less than young, the muscle had softened. Now he had the figure of a domesticated, beer-fed bear. When he frowned two dark creases appeared like the marks of a spoon end. The spoon ends appeared as he saw his wife lying across the sofa in sullen psychic conversation with the bottom of her sherry glass.

'Don't worry, there's more where that came from, you beautiful old soak.' Over he came with a bottle of Harveys Bristol Cream. He propped the little hat at a jaunty angle, standing like a weightlifter in preparation. And then, a one-man circus, Big Oliver strained at the bottle, heaving the cork. It came out with a faint pop. Beth's smile was weak and disappeared. Her glass was refilled. The open bottle went gently on to the low teak table next to a sgraffito pot of white-rimmed ivy.

'What's wrong?'

Beth spread her toes on a sofa cushion, each red nail pressed into the green corduroy. 'Your wife is an idiot, that's what.'

'Everyone knows that, I've known it for years.' Big Oliver tugged the knees of his trousers, sitting next to her on the sofa.

She nudged a foot into his stomach. It bulged, a hard pillow pushing at the shirt buttons.

'I'm big-boned, thank you very much.' Big Oliver gave her a hooded stare.

'Aren't you just.' Also a great lover of food, Beth had a generous figure. 'And they're growing all the time.' The foot prodded his waist. 'Especially here.' She smiled through a sip of sherry.

43

Big Oliver said, 'So, anyway, back to the fascinating subject of you being an idiot . . .'

'Ummm,' she answered, annoyed at herself. 'I was teasing Esther this morning in the library.'

Beth shuffled to sit up, heels propelling her over the cushions to the armrest. Behind the sofa was a room divider – a tall varnished structure of differently sized square compartments, the lower squares containing hundreds of LPs and a set of encyclopedias. She propped her head against the ledge of a shelf which held a spider plant in a red pot and a stack of *National Geographic* magazines. Near Beth, in a square of its own, was a funny wooden animal, a South American animal, perhaps a llama or a goat. It had a wild raffia tail. Beth twisted to grab it, plucking at the tail.

'I was teasing Esther about going on a date –'

Big Oliver's head dropped back against the shallow sofa. '*Beth*, why can't you leave her alone . . .?'

Beth threw her arms up from the elbow, the wooden animal in a fist. 'I can't help it! I'm an idiot! I just want her to meet someone *else*.' More tail-plucking, trying to bend it down. 'Anyway, Es was acting very defensive, very sensitive, as I was talking about her going on a date. And now I remember that it's nearly *the date*.' Beth put the animal on the floor and it fell to its side.

'God,' said Big Oliver. 'Is it?'

'I'd completely forgotten.'

'*Pccch*.' It was a sound from Big Oliver's parachute cheeks. He nipped at the inside of his lip. 'Poor Es . . . two years, bloody hell.'

Beth watched Big Oliver over the rim of her glass.

'Well, why don't we get her to come and stay with us? She could have the spare room for a couple of days.'

Beth considered this. 'Yes, she probably shouldn't be alone. You know how difficult it was last year.'

Big Oliver remembered. '*U'm-h'm*.' It said: I vividly remember.

'She seemed strange today,' Beth said. 'Lonely, I suppose. With-drawn and lonely. I don't know . . . she seemed something.'

'Do you think you can persuade her to come here?' Big Oliver explained his reserve with a lifted shoulder. 'Esther's a strong woman in her quiet, quirky way.'

'I'm a strong woman too,' answered Beth. 'I'll just have to strong-arm her, woman to woman.'

'You are strong,' agreed Big Oliver. He squeezed her arm, pretend-ing to admire it. The arm was relaxed, soft flabby skin. He gasped at the power in her Herculean arm. 'Very strong.'

'And you're strong . . .' said Beth, taking her arm back, '. . . smelling.'

10

Black Pat stood up, the chair knocked around by his huge legs. Esther remained seated. She brought a hand up in order to bite her nails, all of them already hard-chewed. 'Black Pat, what you just said . . . how would I know?'

The kitchen was filled with a luminous gloom. Shadows worked as a clock, informing Black Pat that he was late.

'Right then,' he said, the authoritarian, her question ignored, 'we've got to make a decision.' He corrected this: 'You have, you make a decision. But make it quickly, I've got to go.' He ate more cheese, eating in a gobble to demonstrate the speed he would prefer.

'Please don't do that,' said Esther, wet cheese sprinkling over everything. 'I really hate it when you do that.'

'Do you?' said Black Pat, astonished.

'Please could you stop,' said Esther. 'I really hate it.'

'Do you?' Black Pat said, again astonished, cheese spraying.

It was a form of punishment, this eating. And now enough time had passed, enough tedious wavering. 'What's your decision?'

'Are you going to Churchill?'

This wasn't a decision. Black Pat's tongue moistened the roof of his mouth with slow smacks. Resigned, his haunches hit the tiled floor. Sitting there he was still taller than Esther on the chair. He gave her a display of magnificent disappointment, eyes dull with it. But his delicate senses were in motion. Those instincts sent out

46

frequencies and recorded specks of phosphorescence in the blank screen of Esther's deliberation. Yes, she would make the choice, it was made without her. Secretly he found a cupboard handle behind him and pressed his hip against it, enjoying the massage. The handle snapped off. They both heard it fall to the floor.

Esther was looking at him. His thick neck was almost the circumference of her circled arms. She imagined putting her arms around that neck. With the intuitive memory of muscle she knew that the sensation would be similar to gripping the neck of a horse and feeling it react with shimmering strength. His blackness was radiant in the rising dusk. A handsome spectre, he let her look.

'I can't seem to make a decision . . .'

'Why?' Black Pat's left ear leant in a fold, head cocked.

'Because . . .' Esther said eventually, trying hard to pin an answer.

'You won't let me stay here?'

'I don't know if that's the right thing to do.'

'The *right* thing?'

Esther rubbed a wrist on the tabletop, conflicted. 'I mean the thing that most people would do.'

'Most people . . .' Black Pat made a sassy little move.

'What would most people do?' Esther asked him and herself, mainly herself. 'When faced with this situation, what would everyone else do?'

He said, 'But what do you want to do, Esther?'

Esther didn't know. She didn't believe she knew. She wallowed in a highly melodramatic sort of self-pity. 'I don't know.'

'Yes you do.'

Yes she did. The phosphorescence collected in little pools, gathering. Other glowing points emerged and grew brighter.

Esther wouldn't say it, no she wouldn't. A small poisonous voice slithered through her: yes, say it, Esther. Admit it.

Black Pat played it cool. That colossal physique heaved up, the beefy sound made by four animal legs. The rough leather of the pads on his paws pounded across the tiled floor into the hall.

'I'm sorry, it's just . . .' Esther called after him, '. . . I'm too boring to make this sort of decision.'

From the hall came this reply: 'You're much too honest.'

'Sorry?' She nearly rose from her seat.

A grin burst from the voice: 'I said you're much too modest.' The acoustics changed. Black Pat had mooched into another room and there was silence.

The kitchen was impossibly empty without him. Outside the window a blackbird called with its brisk song. The broken silence healed back together. Soon shadows would grow down the walls as the evening became night, the night becoming late. Esther watched a sad film of herself enduring the dregs of the day, watched herself sitting here over a talentless meal, watched herself from behind as she scraped the food into the bin. And here was the scene where she washed up in socked feet, one sock worked loose and bent under her foot. This sock would flap as she trudged around. Repulsively desperate, the whole scene. Esther made her fingers into a comb, brushing hair behind her ears. A tuft on the crown had been slept on so it rebelled from the rest, not about to surrender now.

The light was greying. A cactus on the windowsill greyed with it. *Another evening with me?* it said. Here in the kitchen, us together.

It was too much, too awful.

She jumped from her chair and made her way to the hall, standing there in the twilight. No dog there. He'd already gone? Quick steps took her towards the front door.

A shape in the dimness stopped her, a shape propped against the front room doorway.

Esther leant back on the wall. 'I thought you'd gone.'

'I can't until I get an answer from you.' Black Pat waited a beat. 'So maybe it's time you said what you meant.'

48

'I honestly don't have an answer.'

A sarcastic scoff: '*Arf.*' His eyes came out at her like horns. 'Maybe it's time you meant what you said.'

'What are you talking about?'

Black Pat shifted, his shoulder hitting the doorframe. 'Listen, how long is it going to take you to make up your mind?'

Esther pushed off the wall and sat on the bottom step of the stairs. Her arm went round the sturdy gloss-painted banister and she shrugged with an elbow. 'How long is a piece of string . . . ?'

Black Pat threw a glance at the clock on the mantelpiece. 'About two minutes.'

'Okay,' she said. It's okay, she said to herself. 'You can stay.'

'De-lovely.' Black Pat's tail drummed the carpet. Dust rose in a mist, beaten from his shaggy tail. He said, 'I've got some bits to put in my new room.'

He sailed out. She could hear him poking round the hydrangeas in the front garden. He came back hugging a cardboard box.

'What's that?' she asked.

'My luggage,' he replied as if she had the intellect of a baby. He carried the box up the stairs. She heard him up there, crashing in the boxroom, then down he came, satisfied.

A nervous laugh escaped. The presumption of his box ready in the garden. 'That was quick.'

He accepted it. 'I'm a professional.'

'But your box was in the garden? You didn't know I'd let you stay here.'

He had a good answer for this. 'A professional prepares.'

She mustered the courage to ask him. 'Black Pat, you can stay for tonight, as a trial run. But, ahm, perhaps you wouldn't mind sleeping in the front room.'

Black Pat made a wet cough from his sinuses, so unimpressed.

'Just for now.' This was an apology. 'I suppose I'll feel safer.' This

49

sounded artlessly rude. 'Sorry, no, I'm trying to say it's only a period of adjustment, that's all.'

Black Pat's tongue slid over the black bulb of his nose. 'Well, at least the front room is better than the garden.'

As an idea, even better. 'The garden? So you'd consider sleeping in the –'

'*No*,' Black Pat interrupted flatly.

'I could put out a blanket and –'

'Forget it!' He walked on hind legs to the front door.

Esther remained on her stair, surprised to feel slightly forlorn at his departure. 'Will you be coming back tonight?'

'Very late.' Black Pat was fiddling with the door lock, finding it hard to grasp. Then he had it, the door opening a crack. Something took his attention.

On the wall next to the front door was a corkboard with hooks for keys. The board was a biography of keys and key rings: a doll's leather sandal from Greece on the car keys; a shell on a chain hung beside a red plastic pendant of a Welsh dragon; a large ornate key hung uselessly, its lost lock long forgotten. Another key held a cardboard room-number tag, a stolen key from the honeymoon suite. Buried in the middle of the board was a key with a wishbone attached to it. From the tangle of countless keys and talismans Black Pat unhooked this one. He stooped to it, the coarse whiskers of his muzzle highlighted as he examined. Esther stretched to see what he held.

To Black Pat's nostrils the scent of the wishbone was still informative, telling a chemical story of pockets and jackets, of frost and rain and humidity. It was a Pantone chart of hormones passed through the owner's hand and linked to the heart.

Esther recognized the outline of the white bone in his paw. She didn't want him touching that key. 'Oh, I forgot to offer you a key. I'll get you a key . . .'

50

Black Pat looked at her quickly, the wishbone replaced on its hook. 'It's all right, I don't need it.'

'You don't *need* a key?' Esther said, disbelieving.

'Nope.'

She watched him. The headlines of her face changed. 'Why did you pick that one?'

Black Pat spoke: 'I've always liked it.' Too explicit. 'I've always liked wishbones, I really like them,' he said, devastatingly unpersuasive, scratching his cheek.

Again he started to go and then was halted by a tone in Esther's voice. She had crept up behind him, seizing the key from the corkboard. They were several inches apart. A dangerous gravity, the strangeness of his proximity fastened her there. Black Pat felt his physicality mesmerizing her, he felt her being spellbound. That gothic seducer, he understood this.

'Black Pat, you'll come back?' Her question wasn't supposed to sound hopeful. It embarrassed her.

His furry head tilted at her, his mouth in a grin she wouldn't yet understand. 'You don't need to worry about that.'

The door slammed.

Minutes went by in the dusk of the hall. The empty house closed around her like a shroud. Esther held the key with wrapped fingers, the wishbone making white indentations in the drumstick of her thumb. It had been Michael's key and so she held it hard, holding it to her chest and protective.

II

9.30 p.m.

'Everyone's downstairs, Mr Pug,' Clementine said gently, trying to coax him into conversation. She stood in the doorway, silhouetted by the warm light of the landing.

The study was a cavern. Puncturing the gloom, a couple of standard lamps illuminated Churchill at his table, sitting with his back to her. The massive mahogany table with claw-and-ball feet had been inherited from his father, Lord Randolph Churchill, the youngest surviving son of the seventh Duke of Marlborough. Heaped across it was a wreckage of photographs, papers and books, all ignored. Churchill sat at this mess, a block of red velvet. He had changed into one of his siren suits, a comfortable man-sized romper with a zip running down the front. Mostly unzipped, a bright vein of white shirt showed through. His hands had abandoned the smouldering cigar stub in favour of pressing firmly on his temples, their pressure causing ridges of skin to buckle.

He was preoccupied by something Clementine couldn't hear, coming from an area near the fireplace. It was a truly disgusting sound, the sound of rocks being chewed so rampantly they would have slashed apart a normal mouth. At Clementine's appearance the source of the noise drew closer to his ears, the chewing accelerating.

'Won't you come down and see everybody?' said Clementine. 'They'd love to see you. Mary and Christopher are here.'

Mary, their youngest daughter, and her husband were regular visitors and good company, but Churchill could hardly hear her now.

The rocks ground together with such speed it seemed sparks would flare from them. They were so near it was obscene. Clementine began speaking again. The combination of noises was intolerable.

'I'll be down in a minute, Mrs Pussycat,' said Churchill, without the usual affection.

'We've saved you some supper. It's chicken,' Clementine said, hopeful.

'It's pointless,' Black Pat said instantly, his voice distorted by a mouthful of rocks. 'We've got things to discuss, you know that.' The thud of a wet rock being tongued out was followed quickly by another. One rock hit the rug, a present from the Shah of Persia, and made a soft noise. The second rock hit the wooden floorboards with a bang.

'I'll be down in a minute,' Churchill repeated with more force. And after fifty-five years of marriage, Clementine knew when to leave him to the thorns of his solitude.

A hole of hushed voices replaced the lively chatter from the floor below as she explained. There was a gap of sad disappointment before footsteps trailed off to another room.

'I know exactly what you're thinking,' Black Pat said, louder now they were alone, his mouth baggy and elastic without a jawful of rocks. 'I always do. We understand each other too well.'

With a grim look over the rims of his tortoiseshell glasses, Churchill began writing. Getting no reaction, Black Pat continued, 'You can't ignore me. We've got too much to do.' A cruel smirk pulled up his muzzle at Churchill's refusal to engage. 'Fine, take your time. I can wait.'

Black Pat moved with heavy, gunslinger steps to the large bookcase behind Churchill, one of many embedded in the walls of the room, and admired a selection of black and white photographs displayed there among the ox-blood and gilt books. One photograph attracted him particularly: an image of Rota, the lion given to Churchill as a cub. The lion had been transferred to London Zoo, where it had matured a luxurious dark mane. Black Pat studied the mane, feeling jealousy itch. Returning the picture, he went over to the aquarium balanced on a seventeenth-century oak chest. Inside were two black mollies.

One vanished behind the weeds. The other came to inspect, its swollen head guided by trailing gossamer fins. Black Pat pressed his tongue against the glass, very keen to eat it, the tongue flattening into a grey aubergine slice. The molly darted away and hid. Black Pat's hot instinct to eat it withered, his tongue leaving a large smear. He slouched back to the fireplace and lay down, making a show of readjusting his giant forelegs several times, the big head propped against them.

Churchill watched this from the corner of an eye. He took off his glasses, holding them in a fist. 'I had expected you to attend the meeting in Westminster this afternoon.'

'I thought about it.'

'Yes.' Churchill massaged his forehead wearily. 'Must we do this tonight? I'm exhausted.'

'I don't negotiate.' Black Pat held his gaze level, cutting into Churchill's tolerance.

On the desk was a cuboid glass paperweight, a miniature cloth poodle set on the top. Churchill put his hand around it, testing the weight. A bronze cast of his daughter-in-law's hand was on the windowsill. He remembered the weight of it, and thought about reaching over. But using this ornament as a missile would probably damage the delicate bronze fingers, maybe smashing them off, and Churchill, fond of the ornament, abandoned the idea. Instead he spoke solemnly, so drained he shut his eyes to draw strength. The dog's ears twitched from the base at his voice.

'You don't negotiate, yes, but perhaps on this occasion you could extend a measure of compassion. I understand that we share a wicked union, and I know the goblin bell which summons you comes from a tomb in my heart. And I will honour my principles, labouring against the shadows you herald. I don't blench from this burden, but –' here he let out a deep breath, laying the glasses down gently – 'it's so demanding; it leaves me so very tired. It would be some small comfort to me if I could ask how long I must endure this visit. Please, when do you leave?'

Black Pat chose not to answer.

With less conviction, Churchill asked, 'Do you leave?'

'*Pffft*,' came the reply. 'You know I can't tell you that. And now we've exchanged pleasantries, let's begin.'

12

Esther lay on her bed, watching nothing. She commanded herself to drop into a deep restful sleep and didn't. Hours had passed since she'd made the sensible decision to go to sleep fully clothed. Now the decision seemed wildly misjudged, staying on the sheets impossible.

Out of bed in a bounce. She reached for the tattered dressing gown, an unattractive thing, yellow and brown paisley flannel and absurdly oversized. But it had been Michael's, so was classified as a treasure. Esther put the dressing gown over her clothes, knotting the belt. Then she shambled around her room looking for a reason to leave, a scratching hand roaming from a shoulder to an ear. It occurred to Esther that food was a good excuse. Eating was as good an excuse as anything. She made her way downstairs to the kitchen, holding the banister through a billowing flannel sleeve.

The bread bin contained the hard heel of a loaf. Esther inspected the heel for mould and then decorated it with a gourmet slop of salad cream. Mud was dried in paw smears on the floor, and some shed fur. Wiping salad-creamed fingers off on the dressing gown, she took a bite. Seasoning might help. The lid fell from the pepper pot when shaken over the mangled crust, pepper coming down in a handful. The emptied pot escaped to the floor, spinning in a curve towards the front room. The bread heel was left to overbalance on the draining board, dropping into the sink.

Not discouraged, Esther remembered an orange and also

remembered sherry. Hacked open, the orange was abandoned after a couple of old dry segments. Knowing sherry should be served in a small vessel, and without one, Esther studied an eggcup. She made an undiscerning horseshoe with her mouth. Sipping from her eggcup, she looked around at the kitchen and found nothing else to occupy her there.

But the boxroom was deeply occupying.

Michael's study was enchanting with its new occupation as a rented room, and it called to her morbid curiosity in an alluring song. Black Pat would be late, he had said as much. And he had agreed to stay downstairs that night. So it wasn't technically his room yet. A verdict was made. Esther refilled her fortifying eggcup.

The door opened to reveal the familiar room. Finding the brown Bakelite switch brought a tent of yellow light from the wicker shade. She looked about her from a place near the skirting board. The single bed was as it had been, neatly made, pillows still fat after their flat-handed beating. Esther reassured herself. It was exactly the same. But staring at the bed, the reality of her decision to let this animal stay in the house threw off its covers of eccentric romance and was revealed as grotesque and naïve. Black Pat under the sheets, his elephantine body on the mattress. The dimensions weren't compatible. Measuring the little bed with her eyes, Esther calculated that the dog would overhang from all edges, a black bonfire of wiry fur and massive limbs, the elbows bent out with hanging paws. His tail, that thick stump, would have to lie in the trajectory of the door.

There on the desk was Black Pat's box. The curtains weren't drawn. Her fuzzy reflection moved across the black window. The box was sealed with tape. She peeled it off, prising up the lid.

Black Pat's possessions were fantastically odd: a clump of brown fur, one side crusted with blood; a rotting log; a hoof from a large deer; a thigh bone, possibly from the same deer, possibly not, its hip sockets licked soap-smooth; a tennis ball foxing with use; a couple of rocks. The wire bin near Michael's desk had been vandalized, the edges crimped with giant fangs.

Needing to organize her thoughts, Esther pulled out the chair and sat. The cushion was a hard lump, her dressing gown in folded bunches around her. Her mind filled with pictures. It was after midnight, this room the last in the house to be decorated and still only halfway painted, Michael in shorts and in disgrace for horsing around, failing to paint more on his wall than a stickman. It was their game and she had laughed at him.

Esther ran her hands over the desktop, feeling the grain. It spoke in Braille of Michael. Different memories; Michael in this room at this desk, long hours in this room with the door shut.

She took a chewed pencil from a ceramic pot to brood on the marks of Michael's teeth. The pencil inspection led into a chance inspection of the carpet along one side of the desk, the area between the desk and the window.

Esther leant into one arm of the chair to puzzle at it. The carpet in the rest of the room was still good, but the weft in this large patch was worn and pilled. She stretched out a foot to examine, scrubbing the crushed fibres with her sole. It wasn't so interesting. She sat up. The pale shape of the absent photograph and its naked nail came into focus.

Staring there, she knew where the photograph was and wanted to see it.

She opened the top drawer on the right of the desk. The drawer made a soundless passage, the photograph sliding into the light on a nest of paper. She cleaned the glass with a flannelled elbow although it was already clean.

It was a picture of their wedding day.

Esther's black and white mouth was open in an upturned laugh at falling confetti. Michael, an arm around her waist, was bending to get into the car, head turned back to grin at someone catcalling from the crowd. The unfastened car door showed a slice of the rear seat, a toppled bouquet of flowers resting on a bottle of champagne lying sidelong in the crease. Behind them the church was visible in pieces, also the gravestones in the cemetery and beds of roses, all mirrored at a different angle in the car window. Flagstones and steps in front of the church were specked with confetti, blown in drifts against the seams of the stone. Surrounding Esther and Michael, the wedding guests were captured in fragments, an arm thrown out here, the top of a balding head. A baby held against a decapitated woman identified Beth, Little Oliver only a few weeks old and in a white cap. The hazy man standing next to her, his cheering face mostly disguised by hands in a funnel, was therefore Big Oliver. A gust of sunny spring wind tossed forward the bobbed hair of an aunt. Leather gloves caught raised mid-clap concealed a female chin and cheeks. And a polished brogue from an anonymous leg was lit with a streak from the chalky, chilly sky.

Esther wedged a knee against the desk edge, rocking the chair on its rear legs. The creaks made a rhythm. The rhythm paused briefly, Esther reaching for her eggcup and finishing the sherry in a throbbing swallow. Standing, she hooked the photograph to its nail, the pale square reclaimed. Admiring it there, Esther wondered why Michael had taken it down and found it troubling. And she wondered why she hadn't asked him and found this unfathomable.

13

2.10 a.m.

Churchill's legs were weighed down intolerably, Black Pat draped over his knees and thighs. The hot, bristly torso was contorted in a way that wasn't comfortable for either of them, the animal stench almost physical at such close range.

Black Pat would not be roused. He wasn't asleep; he was in a state of sullen hypnosis, silently waiting. Churchill couldn't shake him off, the dog heavier than he could bodily move. He was trapped underneath, imprisoned in a maroon armchair. They were in the library. Small and high, the room was lined with bookcases which stretched to the beamed ceiling. Lit with a lamp on the desk, deep angular shadows made caves of the corners of the room. Cooling in the stone fireplace, the blackened remains of a fire was testament to how long they had been there. A brown ceramic walrus guarded the embers from the hearth.

Churchill cut the dog across the back of the neck with the blade of his hand. 'Get off me, you pythonid.' Black Pat didn't move. Churchill struck again, harder. The monstrous canine head twisted round to look at him.

'It's been a hell of a day,' said Churchill.

'You are aware that this day,' Black Pat said, his voice slow and antagonizing, 'is one of several streams bleeding into one of several rivers which bleed into me.'

'Rivers of toxic sediment,' snapped Churchill.

'Perhaps, but the sediment is yours.'

This was ignored by Churchill. He pulled the zip of his siren suit down a few centimetres, as much as the obstruction of the dog would allow. He zipped it up again sharply, creating a small buzzing sound.

Muzzle back against the floor, nose leaching a moist patch into the pattern on the rug, Black Pat said, 'You will retire on the twenty-seventh of this month.'

'Yes.'

'. . . The termination of your career.'

'I'm bloody well aware of it.' A gap and then Churchill's tone was of grim amusement. 'You know, I've thought about my retirement on many, many occasions. And although I never doubted that you and I would meet at this time in my life, on some level I've never lost the forlorn hope that we wouldn't.'

Black Pat closed his eyes, the look of headstone angels.

Churchill continued. 'But here you are as always, bringing with you the crushing torment I can never defend myself against.' His hands meshed, resting on the animal's whiskery back, a back which rose to his collarbone.

'Oh.' Churchill pinched the meat at the bridge of his nose, forcing out the knur of an approaching headache. 'Oh, it's so dire and tedious and so mucksweatingly mundane.' He removed his hand, returning it to nest with the other in the fur. 'I've asked myself countless times why I get stuck, going over and over the years when I can't change anything. The answer is I don't know. I am powerless to stop it. And each time you come here I am again thrown to the jaws of the past.'

The dog's guts rumbled. An embarrassing noise came from his stomach.

Churchill said, 'Eheu! Fugaces labuntur anni.'

'Is that Greek?'

'Latin, you bastard. It means, alas, the fleeting years glide by.'

Black Pat's guts moaned.

Churchill studied a relief model of Port Arromanches in Normandy inset into the bookshelves, its plastic sea a vivid turquoise. 'But I hope you realize that this particular visit of yours is different, that *this* visit is especially cruel . . .'

No response. Black Pat felt the cruelty of his timing in waves of heartache.

' . . . Because I don't have the opportunity to assuage the fears you bring with you any more. I'm about to retire, my work is over. I don't have future work to look to, something I've always relied on to carry me through – the promise that I will do better; that I will mend mistakes; that I will eventually defeat you. Not any longer. This time I am out of time. It is surely a savage thing to do to a man.'

The dog declined answering this. He was uncharacteristically short of sarcastic comebacks. Eyes opening, he murmured into the pile of the rug.

Churchill pressed a thumb on his forehead and leant into it, lost in thought.

Black Pat murmured again, barely a whisper, 'The work you have done is a measure of you as a man . . .'

'I know what you're scavenging for, vulture.'

' . . . And you will be quantified accordingly.'

A deep blast of emotion came from Churchill. 'I admit I feel such doubt about how I will be judged for the work I have done in my life. And now, as I prepare to leave it behind, I feel the uncertainty bearing down on me.'

Black Pat was motionless.

Churchill tapped the dog's fat head. 'Are you listening, you rustic ignorant?'

The fat head didn't move. Churchill stayed quiet for a moment. His voice was fractured when he spoke again.

'Historians are apt to judge war ministers less by the victories achieved under their direction than by the political results which flowed from them. Judged by that standard I am not sure that I will be held to have done very well.'

'No one can help you with this,' said Black Pat.

'What are you insinuating?'

'It is not an insinuation.' Black Pat lifted his face. 'It's an instruction. You know you will not find sanctuary in the answers of others. No peace lies there.'

Churchill said, 'Then let me go to bed.'

The dog's voice was emotionless. 'Have another drink. It'll clear your head.'

Reaching for it, Churchill drained the last of his whisky in retaliation, banging down the glass on a small circular table next to him, the bust of Franklin D. Roosevelt shuddering.

'*There!*'

His head was far from clear, it felt woolly with alcohol and fatigue. The room rocked with the fluidity of oil on water. He blinked to control it, but it rolled on. 'Now *leave.*'

'Not yet,' said Black Pat.

'I'm telling you to leave.'

'Not yet.'

'Then I'm begging you,' said Churchill.

Black Pat's head dropped back to the floor, his muzzle stubbed against the Persian rug. 'I know you are.'

14

4.00 a.m.

The front door closed gently, weight cautiously applied until the lock made a slow snap. Under a powder of sleep in her bedroom Esther was immediately awake. Her eyes swerved to the bedroom door. Open a few inches, the stairhead and landing outside formed a construction of dim shapes.

Noises came from down in the hall, the sound of a lumbering bulk trying not to be heard. There was a dull thud as a shin met the edge of a table hidden in the dark, followed by an agonized pause, the sound of a knuckle bitten to keep from crying out.

Esther lay there as if waiting for an atrocity, a motionless ball.

In the hall there was a tight crack, something plastic being shattered, then a slew of paws, a heavy lurch into the front room's doorframe and a filthy obscenity. Esther shot upright in bed, the sleeves of the dressing gown locked around her elbows, hair thrown over her face. Fighting through the sleeves, she remembered the escaped pepper pot. It would have been funnier, but still funny enough.

Scrabbling claws signalled that Black Pat was scratching at the carpet, the instincts in him to carve out a den. Something ripped. A pounding of paws in a circle was followed by the gradual crash of a body dumping itself on to the floor. Then a sigh came, a peeved one, the head shifting in small posture changes to find a tolerable spot. Bangs came from the head as it lumped around, nothing comfortable.

Esther listened with satellite ears, sitting cross-legged, the bed-covers in chaos. She started to speak and changed her mind. She changed it again and spoke in an emergency hiss.

'Black Pat?'

Another sigh, this time impossibly annoyed. 'What?'

'Are you going to stay down there?'

'*Yes.*' It was the tedious tone of an unresolved argument.

Anxious that Black Pat might invade the upstairs rooms, Esther said, 'You'll definitely stay in the front room?'

'*Ock.*' A snort of contempt. 'Shhh!' A firm demand.

'You'll be there all night?'

'Could you keep your voice down? I'm trying to sleep.'

She did keep her voice down, speaking in a booming whisper. 'Sorry.'

There was no reply, an awkward peace as both of them lay in silence. Esther felt the embarrassment of trying to sleep in the company of acquaintances, that squeak of adult humiliation at talking in pyjamas and then very consciously not talking and lying there in the blackness.

Unable to bear it, she turned on one elbow, twisting to clump the pillows. Her striking fist made a furrow. A few minutes chipped away. From below came the sound of the dog's face lifting to lick at his foreleg with a brusque tongue. Black Pat hummed quietly as he attended the leg. He gargled through the sweeping tongue and it was dramatically unpleasant.

Esther eavesdropped from her bedroom. More repulsive humming. She was reassured. A very tentative reassurance, which strengthened into mild confidence. She experimented with shut eyes until her eyes allowed themselves to remain shut.

' . . . *God.*' Black Pat had stopped, the thing on his leg forgotten. 'I can hear you snoring, you know.' He had something else to add. 'It sounds like a tractor driven by pigs.'

Esther's eyes boggled open, now open for ever. She took sipping breaths with a straw-hole mouth and tried to be noiseless.

Black Pat snickered at the floor and rolled as a horse rolls, heaving his body from the neck. The momentum rocked him over to his other side. With a bluesy grunt he relaxed his muscles into sleep, his ear creasing back to reveal its beef-pink lining.

Thursday 23 July 1964

15

Esther peered over the banister and looked for Black Pat. Not seeing him, she stood on her toes, leaning further, the weight on her stomach. Then, envisioning her death from a collapsing banister, dead on her own stairs, Esther dashed to the bathroom. Locking the door, she went to do the morning analysis of her face. The mirrored cabinet above the green sink described a worried face drawn around a dark migrainous point in the centre. Without ever having worn earrings, Esther imagined earrings and wondered if this would improve things. Now she tried out a grin, grinning at the mirror, changing the angles of her neck.

The grin died in a frown. She noticed an object balanced on the sink's ledge, a stick bound with one of her tea towels. The unbound stick was a wooden spoon, also belonging to her. Esther looked over at the door. The bathroom was suddenly infected with the mysterious and foul habits of Black Pat.

An ear to the door, she heard silence. Maybe he was still asleep? Another problem arose. With clothes still in the bedroom she would have to chance a wet sprint in a towel. Better to get the clothes first, thought Esther. Yes, get the clothes and do the whole procedure in here.

Seconds later she returned hugging an armful of clothes: a mustard cardigan and a cream and blue day dress patterned with kaleidoscope fractals. Screwed up in one prim fist she held a pair of pants. Black Pat turned from the sink. With a thump of cloth everything fell to the floor. Up came his paw, a merry salute. Esther mutely debated the right response.

A patch of the mirror had been wiped clear. Black Pat was holding the wooden spoon, re-wrapped with the tea towel. Rubbing his teeth with it, he worked against the enamel, pushing it around the gullies of his mouth. Cheeks stuffed, he said something unintelligible.

'What?' Esther scraped together her clothes.

He did it again, a string of vowel sounds, an interpretive paw swinging between the sink and the bath. Then he let out a towel mouthful of laughter, a spray of froth landing over the tiles.

'That's my tea towel, I hope you know.' Esther's clothes were in a bundle around the humiliating pants. 'And that's my spoon.' Moodily she said, 'I cook with that spoon.'

He removed it. 'Not now it's my toothbrush you don't.'

'Your toothbrush.' Esther talked disapprovingly to her ankles.

Black Pat developed a disapproval of his own. 'Dental hygiene is important. I aspire to have the smile of Tess of the D'Urbervilles.'

This was intriguing enough. Esther forgot her ankles. 'Tess of the what?'

'The D'Urbervilles. Thomas Hardy wrote that she had a smile like roses full of snow.' He shuffled his head about. 'I paraphrase. It was something similar, perhaps that. Either way, a nice smile.' He lifted the skin of his muzzle to show her, flaunting hooked fangs in a mossy mass, some damp grey, some dappled brown, a few in curving tusks.

Esther took in the exhibition of teeth. No roses of snow, it was a split haggis stuck with shards of coconut bark.

The teeth were put away, the paw repeating its journey from sink to bath, an invitation to use them. 'And if you're going to be late for work please do carry on. I can take a bath later.'

Take a bath in her bath? Esther stared at him with disgust. She stood with a shoulder to the tiles and a solution came to her.

70

'If you want to wash I've got a hose in the garden, I could turn on the hose . . . wouldn't you rather –'

'Pardon?' said Black Pat, pretending at ignorance.

'With the hose, you know . . . a wash. With the –'

'Pardon? You'd suggest this to all your lodgers?'

Esther was careful with her words. 'No, only if they were –'

Black Pat cut her off with a bitchy slant of his eyes. He did it again, a very unsavoury dismissal. A few beats passed and he spoke, the voice patronizing. 'Are you going to take a bath now?'

Esther fidgeted with her bundle of clothes, shifting them around. Black Pat wedged the spoon against his gums. She hadn't answered, so he said the word, 'Okay,' through shut lips. Through shut lips he said, '*Fine.*'

He walked to the tub and manipulated the taps easily. The bath plug was fumbled into place and water began to collect. He squirted a string of shampoo into the rolling water and it foamed. Black Pat squashed himself in, lowered into a torpedo and lunged at the ends of the bath, his front legs flattened, his face thrown over with soap. Colliding with one end, he struggled round and lunged at the other. Water came spilling over the bath sides and collected in lagoons on the floor. Esther refereed silently from above her clothes.

Black Pat tried to clean his back. He overturned and flailed, mouth flooding, his head knocking against the sides. He stood up, looked round at his back, was unsatisfied and overturned again. Then he flipped on to his front and made a few more lunges.

The sight of him there was strangely endearing, working an odd little spell on her. 'Do you need any help?' asked Esther.

'No, just fine,' he replied tartly, eyes buried in soap.

'I could help you.' Esther put her clothes on the wicker laundry basket and fetched a dustpan brush from the cabinet under the sink.

'I don't need any help, thank you,' he snapped, slipping over with a tidal splash.

71

'This method of yours is ridiculous. You look ridiculous,' said Esther frankly. 'Let me help, for Christ's sake.'

Black Pat didn't answer but Esther noticed his lunging had slowed. Now he was floating around gently, paddling his paws. She moved over and started scrubbing his back. The water turned grey as she worked the dirt loose, the bath grey, the floor pooled grey. She scrubbed harder, pumping her shoulders, the brush gripped with both hands. She had to stop now and then to tug her dressing gown back into place.

Black Pat let her rinse him using a plastic cup, which she emptied over him in long sweeps. His face looked mournful as a waterfall ran from his great snout, the bristly hair beaten flat against his ribs. He lifted docile paws like a pony for Esther to clean the pads, then shook them neatly.

The job was done. Esther hung a couple of towels over him, a nice finishing touch. Black Pat stood there, throbbing with the desire to shake his body dry. It was an irresistible urge. His head started turning slowly side to side, lips tight in anticipation.

Recognizing this compulsion, Esther took cover behind the door. There was a second's pause before he began to shake, then a torrent began. Water flew from his coat and battered against the tiles, the towels hurled across the room. It went on until only a litter of specks. Black Pat wheezed with relief when it was over, his fur in tiny spikes.

He stepped out of the bath and puddles grew around him. Black Pat didn't care. He sat down, kneading a saturated ear.

'You weren't really supposed to come up here,' said Esther. 'I thought we'd agreed that you would stay downstairs.'

'I agreed to sleep down there.' He started kneading the other ear. 'However, I'm renting a room up here so I can't be banned.'

'Of course not,' said Esther. 'Not banned. I didn't mean you were banned.' She did. She took in the bathroom: a sodden landscape, a slovenly mess. 'I know you're renting that room.'

'And you pay for what you get,' said Black Pat. He put his weight on one foreleg.

'I think it's you get what you pay for,' said Esther.

'Sure,' said Black Pat. 'It can be that way too.' His smile was a slight one. 'But not in my experience.'

16

Corkbowl walked across Victoria Tower Gardens to Westminster Palace, the river to his right, the banks lined with large plane trees, boats in the water. The grass scratched at his shoes. Victoria Tower rose up. His route took him directly past the Buxton Memorial Fountain, a curious thing of garish coloured arches.

A gate led to a private passage around the Palace, with a flagstone path to the staff doorway. Corkbowl stopped and took a moment to smarten himself up, putting his brown jacket back on over his white shirt, tightening his slackened tie. Then inside the building to the library, the buffeting slip of the double doors taking him to the reception area. Dennis-John was there speaking to Beth in moderated frustration; her elbow rested on the high reception desk.

'When you see her, instruct her that she must report to me. I need to talk to her about an important task.' He added, 'Esther can't spend all her days hiding in corners. It's time she actually *earned* her salary.'

Impulsive reflexes overrode the menace of Dennis-John. Beth couldn't help herself. 'That shouldn't be hard, being as we all earn monkey nuts.'

'And do you know what's worse than earning monkey nuts?' Dennis-John held himself together. Here it came: 'Earning monkey *nothing*.' The genius of this devastated him.

Dennis-John spoke over an invisible Beth. 'Ah, you're here, Corkbowl.' His voice whipped to Beth, Beth again the object of absolute focus. 'Take him, will you? Give him to the reference room.'

Beth pushed off the reception desk, a red grin in a sleeveless shirt-waist dress. On her wrist were blue rattling bangles, an insult to the ears of Dennis-John.

'Loud jewellery,' Dennis-John shot after her, making her halt, 'is indecent in the House of Commons library and will not be tolerated.'

He paused, watching Beth tug off the bangles, putting them obediently in a pocket. Dennis-John made his eyebrows supernaturally judgmental, staring at something. Beth's head swivelled to look at her bare arms, finding nothing. Dennis-John's eyes were on a higher place, drilling at a shoulder. Beth saw a fragment of bra strap. Waiting for her to amend it, Dennis-John said, 'Dressing like the whore of Babylon is indecent in the House of Commons library and will not be tolerated.'

'There,' said Beth, presenting herself, 'I'm completely tolerable.'

'Barely tolerable,' Dennis-John answered. Here came his sly dig at her. 'And this is why it's crucial you work, as it shields your infant son from having to endure the sight of his mother cavorting in her underwear.'

Beth made her standard argument. 'Women can do a lot of jobs, you know, including raising a child.'

'Jack of all trades, mother of none,' replied Dennis-John, a disapprover of these women. 'Just ask your boy, he'll say the same thing.'

Beth turned from Dennis-John and rolled her eyes, used to his insults. They came in such a salad of venom and mad exaggeration that she had to work not to laugh openly. Corkbowl was taken by an arm and led away, much taller than his guide.

Glad to be dragged with her, Corkbowl said, 'You're going to *give* me to the reference room?'

'Yep.' Beth nodded. 'You belong to Dennis-John now.'

'Do I?'

'Don't ever forget it.'

A bit stiff around new people, Corkbowl stared at his walking legs.

75

Beth looked at him, noticing his straight nose, his strong jawline. Corkbowl had a lean long-distance athleticism and an interesting mouth which was small when shut, as it was here. If Big Oliver wasn't around, thought Beth, and smirked. Then she ended the silence. 'You don't say much, do you?'

Corkbowl touched his dark curly hair, the curls springing up under his fingers. The irony of his silence nearly made him comment on it, which he thought would be a snappy debut, except that the moment was missed. No, today he was still only an urbane wisecracking man trapped in the shadow of a man without comic timing.

'Don't worry,' said Beth, catching him with a happy elbow, 'I don't talk much either. I hardly ever say anything, anything ever. I'm known around here as The Mute.'

A joke came from Corkbowl, nearly taking too long to be connected. His soft delivery wrecked any punch. Oh God, he said it anyway. 'Not the whore of Babylon?'

'The mute Babylonian whore!' Out blared a donkey laugh, Beth delighted by this idea. 'Yeah, that's my full title, that's on my payslips. It's what my parents call me.'

They met Esther outside the entrance of room C, a large reading room. She was tying a shoelace, knelt over it next to the heavy wooden door. Hearing their footsteps, she stood up. Corkbowl loafed on the spot, listening to Beth run through her encounter with Dennis-John. Esther had buttoned her cardigan up wrong, two wrong buttons making it pleat on one side. Beth redid the cardigan as she spoke. 'Es, the way you're dressed! What happened to you this morning?'

This morning: Black Pat, the bathroom, the bath with Black Pat in it; his black, wet fur. Esther kept silent, squirming from the nannying fingers under her chin. Beth wouldn't be put off, gripping Esther's waist, forcing her back in place with firm readjustments. Over Beth's hands Esther gave Corkbowl a wordless greeting, an upward shuck of her chin. It said: Oh, hello again. Corkbowl did a similar thing but with more panache.

Beth brushed the cardigan straight. 'Corkbowl was telling me all about himself.'

'Was I?' asked Corkbowl.

'No, but you were just about to,' Beth ordered him, enjoying it. 'So go ahead.'

'Umm . . .'

'Let's start with what you do with yourself.'

'I don't know, really. Ah, I like the normal things.' Anticipating Beth's response, Corkbowl added, 'Normal things like music.'

'You play an instrument?' This was from Esther, interested. A shape caught her attention at the end of the corridor. She looked. It was gone. She checked again. Nothing.

Beth said, 'Esther used to play the trumpet.'

'I used to play the cornet,' Esther corrected. 'Ages ago when I was at school.'

'Right, yes.' Corkbowl moved his spectacles, thick eyebrows behind them. 'I used to play the violin, if that counts.'

'And do you have a secret talent?' asked Beth.

'Not even an overt talent, I'm afraid.'

'What a liar he is.' Beth narrowed her eyes at Esther, a pantomime conspiracy. 'I bet you do, I know you do. I can tell by the look of you.'

'I suppose I cook sometimes. I can cook a few things.'

'A secret chef!' Beth clapped her thigh, the case solved.

'No, ha, not a chef. I can only cook some things, and only very averagely. Only semi-dishes. I'm a sort of semi-chef.'

'A taste of the average with semi-food.' Beth laughed again. 'Magical!'

Yes, and he was a magical man, he told them, having fun. Corkbowl watched Esther's cheeks light with a nunnish smile. He looked

77

at her hair, hair that had never been lavished with attention. A plaster wrapped around the end of her index finger was found to be mystically stylish. Corkbowl's heart rang like a tuning fork.

There was a noise from the reception area, a loud slam of falling books, a female gasp. A vocal assassination from Dennis-John rang off the ceilings, his words a blur through the walkways.

'Whoops. Dennis-John's at high tide.' Beth looked in the direction of the commotion. Her arm pointed in the opposite direction. 'Better give yourself to the reference room, Corkbowl.'

'That way?' Corkbowl pointed with Beth.

She nodded. 'Stay clear of Dennis-John. If you see him, duck.'

Corkbowl was fast, striding off.

'Yes, you can hide but you can't run. If you run you'll trigger Dennis-John's instinct to chase,' Esther called after him. Corkbowl turned as he marched, marching backwards.

Beth had some better advice. 'Just think of him as a peptic ulcer which attacks from the outside. That's what we all do.'

17

1.15 p.m.

Churchill stood at the window of his parliamentary office and took in the view which would soon belong to someone else. Behind him his son Randolph was inspecting the various photographs dotted across the high walls. 'I'm excited about writing your biography, Dad,' he said, one photograph holding his attention, then moving to the next.

'Harrumph,' Churchill answered.

Randolph said something sarcastic under his breath, smiling.

Churchill continued looking out of the window. There was nothing there that interested him particularly. He stared at the branches of a large plane tree which spread into the sky.

Randolph was holding a small ivory elephant, turning it in his hands. 'I don't remember this, is it yours?'

Churchill gave a cursory glance at the elephant. No, it wasn't. Or maybe it was.

Randolph put it back on the cabinet. 'So why are we both in here? I didn't think you had any engagements today.'

Churchill said, 'I don't. My schedule is free. The reason we are here this afternoon is because you are generously humouring your father. It's rather foolish but I felt a strong desire to come to my office, to be here quietly for a while.'

'You'll be here again,' Randolph said gently.

'I don't think I will. And not in this capacity.' Churchill remained at the window, still gazing at the branches. 'No, not in this way again.

If there is a next time it will be different. It'll be different because I will be over the wall, if you follow my meaning.'

Randolph asked, addressing the back of his father's suit, 'Does it hurt you to think of it?'

'Only intimately,' Churchill replied.

Randolph continued watching for a moment, then, wanting to lift the mood, inspected a dishevelled potted plant. 'And what about this wasted thing?' he said to his father. 'Was it always here?'

'I rather think it was,' said Churchill. He grinned at its unhealthy yellowed stem, its straggling foliage. 'I'm not convinced it's supposed to droop like that at the stem. And where are the rest of the leaves?'

'Should we take it with us?'

'My God, no,' said Churchill.

He put a finger underneath his bow tie and stretched it out. The knot was bad and the bow tie came away in a tangled mass. 'Bah,' said Churchill. He tossed the bow tie to a nearby table. It missed. There was a wet smacking noise. Black Pat tongued the bow tie up from the carpet.

'Damnation . . .' Churchill rucked his forehead.

Black Pat chewed the bow tie to the front of his jaws, letting it bunch there. Then he let it hang out, one end flapping wetly. Seconds later it spooled back to the floor, Black Pat finished with it.

'Who are you talking to?' Randolph had turned from the plant. 'Where's your bow tie?'

'It's over there,' Churchill lied; he knew Randolph wouldn't look. He didn't, wandering over to the bookcase and lifting out a large volume, opening it at random and scanning the page.

'Get out, you pill,' Churchill fizzed at the dog. 'I'm here with my son.'

'You're here with your what?' Randolph asked absently from across the room, head bowed to the book.

'I'm here with my thoughts,' said Churchill. 'And my memories.'

'Yes, me too,' Randolph said fondly.

Black Pat was looking at Randolph, studying him with languid eyes. Churchill knew that his son also suffered from depressive periods, seeing the same dark reservoirs in Randolph as were quarried in him. Randolph was free from it at this time, but the sight of Black Pat's expression released a billowing cloud of dread in Churchill, knowing the ebbing and flowing methodology of the dog, knowing also how the spores of his influence could work into your core.

Churchill took up the aluminium shooting-stick he used to aid his walking and moved towards the door.

'You should stay here for a while.' Black Pat's voice was damp. 'Let Randolph go.'

Randolph shut the book with a dull clap of paper. 'Shall we leave now?'

'Let him go,' said Black Pat.

'Yes,' Churchill said to Randolph, and then, 'No, not quite.'

'I'll stay with you,' Black Pat said in a hush.

Churchill strained a note from his chest at what he was about to say. 'Randolph, do you mind waiting outside? I'll be there shortly.'

Randolph left, the door closing with a click. Churchill went to his desk, resting the tips of his fingers on the surface and leaning on them. The desk was well polished, his fingers making small moons of condensation.

He said to the dog, 'I have spent years in this building.' His face turned away. 'I feel my past in the walls and in the rooms. I hear the tide of my existence, the years swelling and then replaced. And the decades draw patterns in foam on the sandstone.'

Churchill moved the position of his hands, ten more condensation moons appearing. The ivory elephant shone white on its cabinet among the gilt-framed photographs. The room was peaceful, its surfaces lustrous in the diffused afternoon light. A wood pigeon called in its passive voice from somewhere close.

The dog was next to him, a black dune. Churchill coughed, making a rough, brisk sound to gather himself, needing to harden up. Head raised, he cast a concluding glance around the office, making a record, eyes finishing at an anonymous spot on the carpet before him. He gave it a few affectionate taps with the end of the shooting-stick, the aluminium giving off a ringing twang. 'So then, this is it.'

18

1.35 p.m.

Esther was busy putting books away, the library trolley at her side stacked high.

A mild Beth appeared. 'I've got a confession to make.'

Around the room were a few politicians, reading and writing at the tables near the windows, none in earshot.

Beth said again, 'I've got to make a confession.'

'Could you make it later? I've got to work. All these books . . .' Esther pointed a thumb at the trolley. 'There's a mountain of them.'

She gave Beth an apologetic smile. The trolley wheels resisted as she pushed. As a strategy to make her stay, Beth grabbed the book Esther had just returned, tossing it back with the others.

'*Beth!*' She forced the trolley into reverse.

'Please, Es, it'll only take a minute.' Beth picked up the book she'd thrown, working it into its notch on the shelves. 'But I've got to speak to you about my confession.'

Beth bullied herself to wait patiently for Esther to ask what she meant. She found herself resistant to bullying.

'Look, I wanted to say sorry for the other day.'

'What other day?'

'Yesterday when I teased you about going on a date . . .'

'Oh, that other day.' Esther twisted her fringe, making it a tube. The tube fell back on her forehead. 'It doesn't matter, Beth. I was being touchy, that's all.'

'No you weren't.'

83

Esther put on an amused frown. 'Hey, there's nothing to apologize for. I honestly hadn't thought about it.'

'That's not strictly true, is it . . . we both know that.'

Esther presented her palms as white flags: you got me. It was a sweet admission. They went to a table, Beth speaking close and low.

'It's nearly the date, Michael's date. I could have smacked myself for forgetting.'

'Did you forget?'

'Not really. You know me, Es, I can barely identify the days of the week, let alone the date.'

Esther clucked her cheek. 'I wish I couldn't.'

Beth delivered her proposal. 'We want to invite you to stay with us, me and Big Oliver. Just until it's over.'

'Oh, Beth.' A feeling in Esther rocked on its base and threatened to spill. 'You don't need to do that.'

'I rather think we do.' Beth was serious, hesitant about what she was about to say. 'I'm probably being . . . I don't know, I suppose I think that . . . I see something in you, just over the past couple of days, and it worries me. You seem very quiet . . .'

'I'm always quiet.'

'Except that no, you're not. And never this quiet, certainly not this distracted. I don't think you should be by yourself.'

'I'm not by myself.' It escaped from Esther. 'What I mean is that I've got you and Big Oliver, so I'm not alone.'

'What about when you're at home? Your parents moved to Devon and you have a tendency to be antisocial, unless Big Oliver and I physically force you, so when you're at home you're alone then.'

'Ha.' Another unintentional sound, hurriedly amended. 'I'm fine, Beth. Thanks so much for your offer, but I'm fine.' She gave Beth a smile of high independence, the Brownie pledge with three fingers.

'You won't come?' Beth wasn't put off. 'If it's because you can't stand the idea of living with Big Oliver I can make him sleep in the car.'

Esther pictured this. She grinned.

'And if it's because you can't stand to live with me I'll make you live with Big Oliver for a while. You'll quickly see your mistake.'

A laugh now. 'You two are so lovely. Especially since Michael . . . you know, since . . .'

Beth scratched into her hair. Her nails collided with a knot and dragged at it. 'I can't believe it's been two years.'

Thoughts of Michael tunnelled through the rubble burial of the past two years. They emerged at a better time, at the times before, at one particular time not far before when they had gone to the Welsh coast. Beth remembered them all on the beach, the octagon of blue shade from an umbrella, escaping towel corners held by rocks; a lifeguard's flag fluttering fast and fierce with a silky sound.

Esther noticed Beth's face. It was the blank stare of an internal cinefilm, that little nostalgic dream. 'Are you thinking about Michael?'

'And all of us. Remember when we played cricket on the beach?'

Esther did: the four of them, pegged to the sand with their thin midday shadows; Beth stood with a hand making a brim, wearing Big Oliver's T-shirt in a curious turban, Esther and her the gossiping fielders. Then a faint thwack, both useless as the ball sailed past; Beth trotting after the ball under wails from Big Oliver as Michael racked up hundreds of runs in his shorts and Esther's floral sunhat; Big Oliver finally tackling Michael to the floor as he morris-danced from the wicket, bat in the air; Beth toeing around in the surf, darting from the ball which rode on cold waves. And then them on their stomachs drinking wine because it was Michael's birthday, patches of the sand red as plastic beakers overturned in a salty breeze; the pouring of wine into a beaker which took off and had to be chased. Worms made spirals of wet sand over the flats left by a retreating sea. Now an exploration to rock pools in the stone cove near the cliffs, the shallow water warmed by an afternoon of sun. Four biologists searched for seaside celebrities, perhaps a crab or a fish, or a starfish, and found burgundy anemones which retracted into balls of liver when menaced by a foot. This was followed by long evenings in the pub, plates and plates and plates of heavy food creating their well-loved expression 'and a salad of chips'.

'Yep, two years. Incredible, isn't it?' Esther was cut off by a new thought, the desire to ask it a hot coal in her. 'Beth, he never talked to you about anything, did he?'

'Who, Michael? Talked about what?'

A politician made an ordeal of twisting in his chair and glaring at them, the chair creaking. Their voices became minuscule.

' . . . Talked about what?'

'I don't know, about what he was going to do? You didn't have any suspicions, never suspected . . .'

'What?' Beth's expression was perplexed. 'Of course not, Es.'

Esther picked through her words and found them to be empty shells. She said it anyway. 'I thought we were happy, Beth. I thought Michael was happy with me.'

'You were happy,' Beth said firmly. 'Esther, it's not a sign of the relationship between you.' She shook her head, positive. 'You know what Michael was like. He was always very . . .' She abandoned the sentence.

Yes, Esther knew. They had talked about it many times, dissecting it.

'Anyway, what made you ask?'

A critical cough came from the window.

'I'm not sure.' Esther turned to the cough and saw an indignant man. His scowl was a low-wattage warning. It will get high-wattage, the scowl said. She was back at her lumpy complaining trolley. The wheels started to give under the persuasion of a persistent hip. Esther whispered to Beth, 'Sorry, I'm not sure why I asked.'

86

'You promise nothing's wrong?'

Black Pat lit in ultraviolet, that great head, teeth. The image flashed and sank. Esther restacked the books, occupied with the task. 'I promise. I think I'm in a bit of a funk.' She corrected it. 'A lot of a funk, actually.'

Beth had an idea. 'Here, I know how to cheer you up.' She passed over a packet of sweets. 'Have a few of these.'

Esther took more than a few and then smiled through a face like a stuffed pocket. Beth poked a round cheek and this nearly ended badly.

'Oh, I forgot to tell you.' Beth gave Esther's bottom a friendly slap. 'Dennis-John wants to talk to you.'

'*Ukh*, Dennis-John.' Esther shut her eyes. 'What about?'

Beth was in the doorway, now in the corridor, her voice recklessly loud. 'Probably something horrible. Better go after you've finished with that trolley. He says he doesn't want you hiding in corners all the time.'

'But I like hiding in corners,' Esther said to the empty corridor.

19

Dennis-John hit his typewriter, striking the carriage return lever. With a shrill ping the carriage smashed to the right. He talked and typed.

'Esther, I wonder if you realize what's happening on Monday the twenty-seventh of July.'

Esther watched the typewriter. The ministry of fingers raged against the keys. 'Umm. I'm not sure.'

'You're not sure.' Dennis-John stopped typing. He shared an indulgent smile with his lap, expecting this answer. 'Then let me explain.' He looked up his forehead at her.

Dennis-John had a dark auburn head of hair, parted to the side. This styling was a never-ending crusade. The hair was wilful and wanted to break out into thick bohemian waves. Sometimes, when Dennis-John was drunk, or feeling beaten, or in a sustained fury, the hair succeeded. For this reason his hair could be used as an emotional barometer by those who knew him. Today the hair was absolutely dominated.

'Monday the twenty-seventh is the date Sir Winston Churchill will retire from parliament. There will be a congregation of national press baying at the doors and Sir Winston will be making a short speech.' Dennis-John waited to see if she was able to comprehend the information so far, faithless in her abilities. Good, the evidence was located. Bravo. He carried on.

'Sir Winston will need to formulate this speech, and will do so in his characteristic style, dictating it in the study of his home in Kent. We need someone meek to be there as secretarial assistance.'

Esther was waiting for it. 'I'm that meek someone?'

'Yes.' Here a grin simmered. 'You're roguishly meek.'

She spoke to Dennis-John's ear, a safer, less explosive part of his head. 'Doesn't Sir Winston have a secretary?'

'His secretary has been taken ill. I received a message to see if I could find a substitute, and I put you forward as I recalled that you worked as a secretary for the MP of an east London constituency.'

'Yes,' Esther said hesitantly. 'Quite a while ago, though.'

'And I believe that you have many years' experience of secretarial positions, yes? You're capable of undertaking dictation, shorthand and touch typing.'

'Isn't there an actual secretary who would be more –?'

'No.'

This was difficult to believe. 'Really? Because –'

Dennis-John ploughed in with his logic. 'It was a personal request from the Prime Minister and I couldn't refuse. The House of Commons library is respected for its dedication to precision and quality. Our devotion to exactitude is legendary, part of the fabric of Westminster folklore. Judged by this folklore the library staff are like . . .' Dennis-John didn't have an example. Now he did. '. . . They're like werewolves for prudence.' Not so great, actually pretty bad. Dennis-John saw that he had to curb the folklore element. His hand switched, ordering her to ignore that. 'So when an emergency calls for a studious, careful individual, they come to me. We're trusted and reliable. And I am therefore trusting and relying on you.' He bobbed his head at her. 'A nice compliment for you, and I am not a man who practises overindulging his staff with praise.'

'Okay,' Esther said. She tried to appear complimented. 'Well, thank you for putting me forward. I'll certainly do my best.'

'Har, you'll certainly do more than that,' Dennis-John corrected. 'You'll aspire to do *my* best. Anything less than that, the inadequacy of *your* best, is completely inappropriate. Do you understand?'

Dennis-John observed Esther, searching for proof that she had understood. Yes, there it was. A new statement needed to be expressed.

'Esther, Churchill is not a man to suffer fools, so be careful to act with this in mind. Don't make any girlish comments. Don't ask stupid questions, and to clarify, *all* questions will be stupid. Don't use less than double-spaced lines. Don't giggle –'

'I don't think I ever giggle,' Esther cut in. 'I definitely don't do it much.'

'And a man of Churchill's age has earned the right not to have his day of rest overly disrupted. For the sake of speed you will take Sir Winston's dictation straight on to a typewriter, as his secretaries did in the war. So don't bash the typewriter, don't bash at it.' Dennis-John remembered something. 'Although he only uses Remington typewriters, a specially adapted version imported from America and designed to be noiseless.' He checked himself. 'However, this is not an invitation to type like an ape.'

'I won't do any ape typing,' said Esther, and then, 'Gosh, noiseless typewriters?'

'And . . .' Dennis-John didn't enjoy talking to his staff about delicate matters, especially his female staff, fearing crying scenes. He thought Esther looked like an easy crier. But looking at her he knew the subject had to be broached. He advanced on it without further delay, charging it. 'Esther, it's essential to present yourself presentably.'

Esther considered what he meant, didn't know, and asked.

His thumb sought the area under his chin, stroking it. It was the motion used to get a cat to swallow a tablet. 'Be presentable. The way you are now, with that outfit –' he swallowed his tablet – 'it's in need of revision. The outfit needs fundamental revision.'

She stared down at her clothes, down at the brown brogues water-faded in patches, stockings in grooves at the ankle.

Dennis-John noticed her pinching at her thighs, trying to hitch the stockings through her skirt. 'You can't go to Churchill dressed in your usual jumble sale finery.'

'My jumble sale finery . . .'

'Esther, it is not –' Dennis-John shook his head twice: two epic sweeps – 'is *not* acceptable attire for such a serious, momentous occasion in the presence of such a serious, momentous man. So smarten up, yes?' He had a further suggestion, dealing it out. 'You could even risk a foray into cosmetics.' A hand moved around his face in a circle. 'You know, the pastes women carry in their handbags . . . the pastes . . .' The hand rotated as he searched for the names, mentally ransacking the products his wife used. He found one: 'Rouge! Like rouge.' Dennis-John finished his efforts. 'Go and talk to your painted friend Beth. She'll know.'

Esther remained in front of him. Half of her wanted to leave, sick of his rude commands. The other half wanted to stay for this reason, entertained.

Seeing her there dry-eyed, Dennis-John congratulated himself. No crying scenes. With unnaturally generous sympathy, he said, 'Listen, Esther, no one's expecting you to compete with Elizabeth Nel, but you'll have to get over that because I'm confident you can make a decent job of it. Churchill isn't difficult – he's simply specific in his secretarial requirements. So just remember: do everything right, do it silently, paste on some rouge, wear something coherent with other women your age, no apishness.'

'Who's Elizabeth Nel?'

Dennis-John wasn't through with his list: 'Don't even think about joking. If I find you've been making any jokes, japing around, I'll take more from you than your job.'

'I don't think I'd have the nerve to make any jokes.' Esther imagined it. 'And if I'm honest I'd be too nervous to laugh if he told me a joke.'

'You will laugh should Churchill tell you a joke,' said Dennis-John. 'You'll laugh instantly, and for a courteous amount of time.' He waggled his mouth, deciding. 'For ten laughing seconds.'

'Sorry, who is Elizabeth Nel?'

'Ah,' said Dennis-John. 'Elizabeth Nel. She was a wartime secretary, a celebrity in the secretarial community. Nel was with Churchill on VE day, taking his final night's dictation. A true professional and a favourite of Churchill's. Anyway, we will send you down to Chartwell on the afternoon of the twenty-sixth. That's a Sunday. You'll be needed for approximately one hour or so.'

'Sunday?' Sunday: it came over her in a snowfall of soot. Esther couldn't explain it to him.

Dennis-John saw her basset-hound expression. A classic malingering expression.

'Transport.' Dennis-John thought of the obstacle and crashed through it. 'We'll send someone down with you, someone to drive you.'

'I could drive myself? I have a car so I could easily –'

'What you'll easily do is get easily lost in the miles of rural roads. Chartwell House isn't on your bedside table, Esther. It's in the countryside of Kent.'

A click of fingers from Dennis-John, calling to another female library clerk. 'Hey! I need you to get me whatsit . . . that new library clerk called . . . him, the new . . .' Another flurry of clicks came, first as research and then as the answer. 'Yes, get me Corkbowl.'

The woman went, back seconds later. Corkbowl came, acting the serious professional to impress Dennis-John. He shot Esther a furtive grin and she smiled.

Dennis-John wanted to know, 'Can you drive?'

He could. He owned a cream Morris Minor, the glove box stuffed with rubbish. Corkbowl scratched at a cheek and there was the sound of stubble.

'You'll be accompanying Esther to Chartwell House on Sunday afternoon. Corkbowl, I assume you're a competent driver?'

Esther mouthed, 'Sorry,' at Corkbowl.

Dennis-John didn't wait for a response. He was typing again, head bent.

'You should be,' Corkbowl mouthed back.

'Esther, work!' barked Dennis-John, watching her with psychic powers from his scalp.

20

2.55 p.m.

Clementine was in the kitchen garden, pulling weeds from around the parsley. She picked some mint, bruised the leaves between her fingers and breathed it in. A large orange cat basked near her, swatting the ground with its tail. Then the cat's ears flattened back and it hissed.

'Jock, behave yourself.' She turned to see Churchill slowly advancing across the lawn towards her. Not long back from Westminster, he walked up through the orchard of pear and apple trees surrounding the lake. The orchard led in a path to the kitchen garden, where it connected with a stone archway. Black Pat, trailing behind Churchill, noticed the cat and picked up the pace, overtaking. The cat pressed down on to its stomach. As they got nearer it gave a livid squall and shot off, vanishing over the high brick wall Churchill had built himself.

'I don't know what's got into him,' Clementine said in surprise.

'Who knows,' said Churchill, knowing exactly, watching as Black Pat moved over the cat's scent, nose to the ground and burning to give chase. Black Pat restrained himself, sitting next to Clementine, his back to her. Clementine pulled her shirt tighter. 'My, I just caught a cold breeze.' She looked at the brilliant sky. 'There's a real chill suddenly, how curious.'

Churchill kicked at the dog, catching him hard in the side. He went to kick it again but Black Pat jinked out of the way. Clementine let her shirt go. 'Ah, that's better. It's warmed up again.' She weeded as she spoke. 'So how are you feeling today, Mr Pug?'

'Oh, you know, Mrs Pussycat. Not so bad.'

She didn't look up from the plants. 'Now you mustn't lie to me, Mr Pug. I know Monday must be playing on your mind. Don't you want to talk about it?'

Churchill surveyed the distance. Black Pat threw his head round, assessing what Churchill was looking at, and saw it wasn't anything.

Churchill passed a hand over his scalp. 'It's nothing, Clemmie. I'm just being doomy.'

'Come on, Winston. Tell me.'

She stood up, a woven basket full of fruit over one forearm, and offered Churchill a strawberry. He stared at the strawberry sadly, picking at the stem as he spoke.

'It feels indulgent, but I suppose my father is on my mind a great deal these days. As Monday nears I seem to think about him more and more often. I would have liked him to live long enough to see I was going to do some good. I dearly wish I knew that he thought I had done well.'

Clementine's tone was kind, knowing the difficult spectre of Lord Randolph Churchill across Winston's life, its ceaseless presence. 'I'm sure he would be very proud of you. I'm sure he was very proud of you when he was alive.'

'I don't know about that,' said Churchill. 'I feel so uneasy about everything. I can't bear to think of it. It's exhausting. All I want to do is lie doggo until it's all over, to frowst in my bedroom.'

'Stop that.' Clementine put her hands fondly on his shoulders, the basket swinging on her elbow. 'You've worried yourself into a hole and I won't allow it. You must talk to me about it, I insist.'

'I know, I know.' Churchill turned the strawberry over. 'It's pure baboonery on my part.'

'Baboonery at its absolute purest, yes.'

Black Pat was upright on his back feet, dwarfing Churchill. A rough front paw swatted the strawberry from Churchill's hands.

The strawberry fell. A hind leg came out and ground it into a red spot on the grass. Churchill glowered with barbaric eyes. Black Pat said in a flat, moronic whisper, 'Heh-eh-eh. Heh-*eh.*'

Hearing Churchill growl, Clementine looked quickly to see what he was frowning at, appeared to see nothing, and set about collecting her gardening tools, the fruit basket placed on a garden chair. Finished, Clementine looked at the pulp curiously. 'Winston! That was a perfectly fine strawberry.'

'There was a beetle . . .' Churchill said hastily. 'It caught me by surprise.'

Clementine cuffed his arm, smiling. 'A beetle? Don't be so silly. Now won't you come in for a cup of tea?'

'Ah.' Churchill exhaled heavily. 'I suppose so, I suppose so.'

'Winston, you're a good man. A *good man.*' Clementine smiled directly into his face, arresting his gaze, seeing buried between the years the younger ginger-haired man who had pursued her. 'And as a good man you deserve a cup of tea *and* a slice of cake, perhaps even two if you pull yourself together. How's that for an offer?'

21

6.20 p.m.

At home Esther levered off her stained brogues with her heels, kicking them away. A distracted singing came from the kitchen. The parquet floor in the hall was marked with soil, something she noticed as she walked, the singing becoming clearer. A pain in her foot made her lift it up to inspect, wobbling on one leg: it was a sharp piece of gravel, gravel dotted around, now a hole in her stockings.

Black Pat sat at the kitchen table, playing patience with the deck of ancient cards that lived in the sideboard. A vase from the window-sill was on the table, the flowers emptied into the sink. Black Pat took a finishing swig from the vase, singing through his swallow. He poured in more beer from the bottle next to him. He started to sing again with a crooning tilt to his forehead. 'A bone in the fridge may be quite continental, but diamonds are a girl's best friend.'

'In the popular version Marilyn Monroe sang about a kiss on the hand,' Esther said, slipping to the fridge.

'Talk to me, Harry Winston, tell me all about it!'

Esther turned with a hand on the fridge door. 'If that's a Marilyn impression, you've made her sound like something from the crypt.'

Black Pat made a playful face at the cards, this conversation fun for him if not for anyone else. 'Well, we all lose our charms in the end.' Bothered by an itch, he shook his massive head, plush ears smacking against his skull. The bottle of milk in the fridge door was reached for and then forgotten as Esther confronted a giant bone squatting there on a baking tray.

'*Oh my God.*' She bent into the fridge. 'What's this?'

'A pineapple.' Black Pat checked over a shoulder to receive appreciation for the joke, a scene for canned laughter. No laughter, just a cold wait for an explanation. The cards clapped down. 'It's a bone, obviously.'

'Yes, but what is it doing in my fridge?'

'Causing a crisis.'

Another joke was wasted on this unresponsive audience.

A paw reached out, claws beckoning. 'Look, the crisis is easily solved, give it here.'

Esther handed it over and Black Pat made a ravenous noise. He cracked at the bone with the egg-sized molars at the rear of his mouth. An eye tightened in a squint. The bone crushed into fragments. Black Pat's muscular tongue worked to get at the marrow inside. Splinters scattered over the table and cards, teeth grating. A quick pause for inspection aroused his appetite and the mauling resumed. Esther got a glass of water, the first sip taking her to a chair on the opposite side of the table.

Black Pat had hollowed the bone into a pipe now, both ends ground off and the marrow emptied.

'That's quite unlovely to watch,' Esther said.

'Don't watch then,' said Black Pat. 'Shut your eyes.'

'I will still be able to hear you doing it.'

Black Pat put his lips to the bone and jeered down the pipe at her: '*Booo!*'

His muzzle was crusted in a dark substance. She peered at it. 'What's that on your face?'

'Blood,' he replied straightforwardly. He saw her expression. 'Mud?' Was this better? . . . It didn't seem to convince her. Then he said, 'What are you doing this evening?'

'Oh, I don't know.' She debated with the water, swirling it in her glass. Some splashed out. She dried a hand on her thigh. 'Probably what I do every night. Nothing much.'

'I thought so, yep.' Black Pat was on his hind legs, the beer vase squeezed in an elbow. The bone was a tour guide's baton, held to the back door. 'Follow me.'

The rosy gold garden yellowed in the late sunlight, midges and little insects yellow specks. There in the centre of the lawn, a collection of stones and bricks, on top a tray badly fashioned from chicken wire. Underneath burnt small, snapping flames.

'A fire?' Esther sprang towards it.

'I've built,' Black Pat announced it with a ringmaster's arm, 'a *barbecue.*'

'It'll burn the grass!'

'Who cares about the grass?' said Black Pat.

Resigned, Esther sat on her knees and prodded the fire with a slim twig. The lawn around it was scorched. It prickled through her stockings, the blades made tough and pale by the sun. Esther shifted on to her bottom, taking a look at the gravel hole at her foot. She stretched her legs out, rocking her ankles and enjoying the blanket heat of the evening. Black Pat was busy with a shrub near the fence, one paw scooping through it. The paw found an object and Black Pat slammed his head through the foliage. A pillowcase in his teeth, he came up. Esther looked at Black Pat, not delighted to see the pillowcase.

This pillowcase, it was immediately apparent, had been stolen from the pillow in the boxroom. And it contained something, a swinging bulge inside.

Remembering the tea towel and the spoon, and already rinsed with the futility of arguing, Esther said, 'That's my pillowcase you've buried in the garden, I hope you know.'

'I've organized this as a surprise for you, I hope you know,' Black

Pat answered. 'It's not every day you get surprised with a barbecue . . . or by a barbecue.' He smirked at the lump in the pillowcase as it swung.

'What's in there? Is that something else I own?'

'Nope.' Black Pat upturned the case. A small bald shape fell out, crudely plucked and gutted. Two legs showed it was a bird with a pair of oversized feet. He picked it up, dangling the bird by a naked wing.

Esther wanted to leap up but not enough to actually do it. 'What are you going to do with that?'

'This,' said Black Pat, tossing the wing. The bird landed with a sizzle on the wire tray.

Esther inched over to inspect. 'What sort of bird is that?'

'Not sure,' said Black Pat, now the chef, poking the bird on to another side with a stick, then drawing it back. Fat dripped into the flames and sparked. 'It wasn't flying when I got it, but that doesn't mean it couldn't fly.'

'Where did you find it?'

'Near a pond, it was standing near the water.'

'What colour was it?' Esther made the beginning of a diagnosis.

'A bit white on the beak, mostly black.'

'Black Pat, was it a coot?'

'Coot.' He experimented with the sound of the word, finding it amusing. 'A coot.'

'You're cooking a coot for us?'

'Not us, you. I'm cooking it for you.'

The coot had performed a rotation, the wire tray uneven. It was about to topple from the grill, but Black Pat stabbed it back with his stick.

A selection of other corpses were piled discreetly further up the lawn, all spatchcocked by that butchering mouth. Was that a heron? she asked him.

'Heron?' he repeated, no authority on bird breeds.

'How many birds did you kill?'

'Dum-de-dum,' Black Pat answered in a breathy song, ignoring her. Then finally, 'Don't worry, none you knew personally.'

Esther had a new thing to examine, a horse chestnut leaf next to the fire, the wide green paddles ready for service. Probably cooked, the coot was barged to the edge of the barbecue. Black Pat's stick knocked it off. The coot rolled to a stop on the grass. Black Pat jabbed it on to the leaf plate. Trickier than expected. He punted it with a hind leg. Esther wouldn't see. Yes she did.

'There, that's for you.' Black Pat performed a medieval bow.

Unpleasant: 'Just me?'

'Bon appetite.'

'Appétit,' Esther corrected.

Black Pat's final correction was uninspired. 'Bon eat-it-up.'

The coot's heat had wilted the leaf. Esther drew it to her and a section ripped loose. The bird was revolting. She pushed a finger at the hot meat. She cleaned the finger on the grass. Feeling Black Pat watching her closely, Esther twisted a drumstick. The coot held together. Black Pat's anticipating eyes gave her no alternative. She lifted the whole bird by its leg and dared herself to bite it. The drumstick went to her mouth and then retreated. She brought it back and then moved it away. Here it came, another try. No, hideous, it wasn't possible.

Black Pat had wanted some gratitude. What he got was this babyish ingratitude. In a gesture of magnificent clemency he let out a little canine whine. It was an invitation for the drumstick. Glad to be rid of it, Esther threw the coot over. He blocked it with his neck and the coot did a wild rebound and lobbed into the bushes. Black Pat went after it, couching in the flowers, mashing them beneath him with a green popping of stalks.

'Please don't do that,' said Esther. 'You're destroying my plants.'

'Am I?' said Black Pat, the idea incredible. More stalks popped. A lunge from the waist did this on purpose, the bushes shaking and crushed.

'You *are* destroying them,' Esther said, the moody narrator.

'Am I?' Such an irresistible game. He ended it, emerging with a hiking shoe in his mouth.

The brown leather had split with age, old dirt caked on the sole. Black Pat pitched the shoe on to the barbecue. Wood collapsed from the main frame in a flare of orange ashes. He moved around the fire and blocked her view.

'Whose shoe is that?'

'Mine now,' he answered. A big sheet of smoke, the smoke of a blazing shoe, hit them. Esther shuffled from the smoke on her heels and hands. Black Pat used a stick to dig through the tangle of burning laces, the shoe cooked. A quick, thumping paw stamped out the embers and he lay with his back to her in the dusty trough beside the bench.

'Are you really going to eat a shoe?'

'Are you really asking?' It was an original and difficult pronunciation, mouth crammed. He pinned the shoe with his claws and ate with the pigging guilt of a thieving dog.

'Why are you eating like that?'

An ear rotated. 'Like what?'

'Like you're trying to eat in secret . . .'

Black Pat nudged himself round. He watched with the haze of his outer sight as Esther studied the shoe. And she recognized it in a wave of familiarity.

' . . . Black Pat, that's Michael's.'

He lowered his apologetic nose.

'You stole it from the shed?'

The shed was a gracefully rotting structure at the shady end of the garden. Padlocked, it contained the lawn mower and other tools, packets of fossilized seeds and a stack of pots with the bloom of old terracotta. This shoe was from a pair worn by Michael. He had worn them when it rained, when he and his wheelbarrow had an engagement with manure; he wore them during autumn bonfires, laughing at Esther and Beth's puckered faces as they braced for fireworks.

'You're eating Michael's shoe.' Esther's voice ran with warmth for the shoe. Her thoughts bucketed around the parameters of the coming anniversary. Black Pat was baiting her and she was afraid of the intention behind it. But then this was replaced by a type of flaccid affection. He was her disgusting companion. Company, it was company.

Oblivious, Black Pat clawed a morsel of leather from his teeth. He choked something up and then swallowed it down. He put his head on the ground. A gluttonous intake of breath made something catch in his throat with a '*Hyup!*' The cure was a hacking cough.

Esther stood up, the soles of her stockings brown with soil.

'Where are you going?' called Black Pat.

'To get a gin and tonic.'

'Can I have one?'

The joking hostility was only partly joking, the wound of Michael's eaten shoe still red. 'Why should I let you?'

'Because, because, because, because, because,' Black Pat said to the tune from *The Wizard of Oz*, speaking in a song, 'because of the wonderful things I does.'

A curt response came from the kitchen doorway. 'Everything you *does* is horrible.'

'Stop being,' Black Pat called after her with a rich grin, 'so flirtatious.'

In the kitchen Esther made herself a drink. She selected the plastic watering can from under the sink for Black Pat, making a cocktail ten times bigger. Back in the garden she saw he had performed a vivisection on the shoe remains, taking it into separate parts and dealing them out in a fan of bits. A surgeon, Black Pat pored over each leather organ.

Esther's toes scrubbed around, disturbing the display.

'Is that watering can for me?'

'No, me obviously.' Esther's serious face was betrayed by a smile. Handing him the watering can, she said, 'It's absolutely ideal for you, admit it.'

A dubious solution, Black Pat took it anyway. He had drunk enough beer, the effect in him being an ambitious embrace of novelty. He pushed the nozzle down his throat, sucking at it like a foal, and bowled his eyes at Esther. The look was an exclamation mark, a victory for novelty. But he was serious when he next spoke.

'You can talk to me, you know . . . if you want.'

'About what?'

A cautious pause: ' . . . About him.'

Michael? Esther said, 'Why?'

'Because he was nice,' Black Pat answered. He heard himself. 'He must have been . . . You did marry him.'

Esther had this to say: 'Yup.'

'So talk to me.'

A period of silence clipped past. 'I can't.' She said it again, to him and herself. 'I can't.'

Soft and ulcerous: 'Esther, you can.'

And she practically did. But the hood came down. 'Well, I don't want to, so you'll be waiting a long time.'

Black Pat was quiet for a moment, feeling the electricity that blossomed from the little casket of Esther's chest. He lay there, feeling it. Then he said with a violating intimacy, 'I can wait.'

22

'I got this from the tree at the bottom of the garden,' Big Oliver said, striding through the French windows into the dining room. In an Olympic torch hand he held an apple. 'From the garden!' he repeated, looking at the apple as if it was the first on earth. He took a bite and a chunk with core and pips came away. 'Christ,' he said, sharpness pinching his face, 'that's *sour*.' The apple was abandoned on the table.

'I've had an idea,' Beth announced to the pages of last week's newspaper.

'Oh yeah?' Big Oliver landed heavily on the sofa.

'Esther doesn't want to stay with us, but –'

'She doesn't? Did you keep trying?'

Beth chucked the paper to the floor. 'It didn't work, but I've got a plan.' She told him about Corkbowl. He was an intriguing find, she explained, with excellent credentials; tall and charming. And as if being a tall charmer wasn't enough, he could also potentially be a counterpart to some of her single female colleagues; she couldn't think who exactly, no, it wasn't as though she had anyone in mind . . .

'Cork what?'

'He's only just started working at the library. I'm going to invite them both round to lunch.'

'You know,' Big Oliver was in discussion with the ceiling, 'I feel like we've had this conversation before, literally yesterday, about you shoving yourself into Esther's love life and it turning out badly.' He glanced at Beth. 'Isn't that weird?'

'No, it's nothing like that, nowhere near anyone's love life. This is an innocent meal with friends.'

'Friends like Cork man.'

'Cork*bowl*. I thought I would invite him as a precaution. He'll force us to have fun.'

'Why wouldn't we have fun?' A realization. 'Hold on, when are you planning to have this lunch?' Big Oliver groaned, the answer obvious. 'Sunday? Oh, Beth.'

'So you see, having Corkbowl around will stop us moping.'

'Don't you think we're allowed to mope?'

'We all miss him, of course we do, but missing isn't the same thing as moping.' Beth leant her head. 'It's been two years, Big Oliver. Michael would hate us being like this, Esther especially. And don't think he wouldn't give you a hard time for it.'

Big Oliver wasn't convinced. 'I'm still not really sure it's a good idea.'

Beth weighed it up. 'Rubbish, it's a great idea. And anyway, what else is Esther going to do? At least she'll be here with us.'

'But on *that* day, Beth? On the day of Michael's . . . on his, you know.'

Beth's foot went down on the newspaper and rustled it. 'It might take Esther's mind off it all – give her some relief, even if it's only for a short time. I'm worried about her. She seems . . . I can't explain it . . . she seems like Michael.'

'Michael?'

'Sort of. When he was moving into his . . . when it started on him and he . . .'

Big Oliver put an arm round Beth's shoulders and jostled her. 'Okay, okay, listen, what about if you talk to her about the lunch, just mention it in a casual way and see what she makes of it. You never know, I could be wrong and she wants to do it . . .'

A pause of analysis. 'You have been wrong before.'

'Frequently.'

'Constantly.' Beth was quietly persuasive. 'You're also an idiot.'

Big Oliver said, 'That's what they say in some circles.'

'And if you take advice from someone you believe is an idiot, who's the bigger idiot . . .'

'That's what they say in every circle.'

A smile appeared and then amplified. Beth said, 'So that means I probably should ask Es if the idea's stupid before we totally disregard it.'

'U'm-h'm.' Big Oliver nodded in a gesture of measured consent. 'I suppose we may as well get Esther's verdict on our stupidity, because then we'll have evidence that we are completely stupid, and we'll be proved right.'

'Perfect, perfect,' said Beth, always a pervert for bad odds. 'I love being proved right.'

23

'God in heaven, you stink,' Churchill said without looking up from his book. Lying in the hot bath his body was the pink of a boiled gammon. The evening had gone undisturbed so far. And now the dog had clumsily reappeared near the linen closet. He reeked of alcohol and strenuous physical effort.

Tears of condensation wept down the night-blackened windows, the bathroom filled with steam. 'We quite enjoyed your little hiatus,' Churchill said, turning the page. 'I had expected you earlier.'

'I had another appointment,' Black Pat said, slurring his words and regretting the amount he had drunk. 'Sorry 'bout that.'

'No need to apologize, you bushy popinjay,' Churchill said. 'Your company is never much appreciated around here.'

Black Pat didn't answer at first. Then said, 'I had a barbecue to attend.'

Churchill turned to look directly at him, amazed, water sloshing over the tub sides on to the tiled floor. 'That explains the stench of foul liquor, although I wouldn't have thought it was very professional to drink on the job.'

'It wasn't a job,' Black Pat replied. He sniffed delicately at Churchill's slippers until Churchill's book caught him on the side of the head. Churchill said to the dog, 'You're telling me you were invited?'

He answered pretentiously, 'I would hope so, being as it was my barbecue.'

The absurdity of it forced Churchill to smile. It was a tart, unwelcome smile. 'Well, well, well.'

Black Pat went to make a pithy comment but caught one of his paws and pitched into the towel rail, dragging towels down over him.

'You're drunk!' Churchill broadcast to the room, watching from over the rim.

'And you're naked,' Black Pat shouted through towels, trying to remember the quote. 'But in the morning I will be sober.'

'Obnoxious guinea worm. In the morning I will be clothed,' Churchill shot back, retreating out of sight into the water. 'But you will always be a bastard.'

24

3.00 a.m.

Esther awoke with a gentle jolt. The primitive departments of her brain, the units that dealt with anciently evolved instincts, were wiring encrypted telegrams to her consciousness. They told Esther in a subtle siren that Black Pat was near. The sirens were insistent, he was very close.

It took a minute of hard concentration as she listened through the shades of silence, but then it came. Underneath the sound of the sleeping street, the sound of her own breathing, was the ambience of an animal. Esther stared at the bottom of her bedroom door, at the gap there.

The light in the porch was always left on at night, drawing a thin line under her door. Not tonight. The door strained in its frame, a weight barricaded against it.

An edgy chewing of her inner cheeks. Esther tried to think of something appropriate to say.

'Are you comfortable out there?'

Black Pat spoke with his chin on the carpet. 'Compared to what?'

So he was lying by her bedroom. It was nothing. If it seemed to have an aftertaste, then Esther decided this was surely the work of an inventive mind. They talked with late-night voices through the shut door, mumbles in the hinterland of dark, and her inventive mind got the better of her.

'Do you know,' she said, playing the casual observer, 'I'm finding your being there a bit –'

Black Pat's answer was ridiculous. 'Beatnik?'

'No, I was thinking more that it's a bit creepy.'

'Not beatnik?' Black Pat didn't believe it.

'It is quite unconventional.' She gave him that. 'And also quite . . .' Should she say it? She said it: ' . . . Quite unconventionally creepy. Quite a lot. Really a lot, actually.'

'Nah.' Black Pat had the tone of innocent denial, firmly innocent. 'I'm just an old hound dog trying to get some sleep.'

'Right outside my door when I'm in bed? Couldn't you be an old hound somewhere else?'

Black Pat shifted his waist, the cathedral of ribs aching from the bare floor. A chime of pain from his shoulder blade made him say 'Ooch,' and nurse it into another position. He said, 'Well, I hope you're happy in your bed, your skeletally collaborating bed. This floor is . . .' Out came a tinny whine. 'Could I come in there with you?' He made a puppyish, earnest little noise.

Esther made a gagging face at her wardrobe, disgusted. 'No. Absolutely . . .' She searched for a word. She settled for this: 'Ugh . . . Yugh.'

Both parties retreated. A quiet grinding on the other side of the door made the party in the bedroom suspicious.

'Are you eating something?'

'I am not,' said Black Pat, filing his teeth on a sheep's pelvis he had rescued from a ditch. The sumptuous taste of decayed bone; he gnawed a loving hole in one edge, scrubbing his tongue into the cavity. He let out his puppyish whine again. 'Please let me come in there with you. Please, Esther . . .'

'Go away.'

'Even though the floor's too –' He hit the floor with a paw, a punishing blow. 'But I'm not allowed in,' he said sadly, so very sorry for himself. 'You won't let me in,' he said again, such a sad dog. There was a subtle transformation, oblongs of streetlight moving across his eyes. He said to the pelvis in an inaudible slip of breath, 'Yet.'

Friday 24 July 1964

25

Beth was wearing a raspberry dress with a white zip on the front, a white cardigan slung in a rope over one shoulder. Beth slowed down to skim her coffee to a manageable level, then sped up, heading to a table in the centre of the staff canteen.

Hooking the leg of a chair with her ankle, Beth sat opposite Corkbowl. He made a welcoming sound over a mouthful of flapjack and shut his newspaper. He did the universally understood spin of his hand to show he couldn't understand why it was taking so long to swallow. It was the spin that said: I'm bored of chewing; I can't believe I'm still chewing.

Beth broke off a corner of the flapjack. 'Guess what you're doing for Sunday lunch.'

'Something unexpected?' Corkbowl answered. He had another guess. 'Something to do with you?'

'Bingo.' She looked at the newspaper's front page and then wasn't interested. 'I'd love it if you could come for Sunday lunch.'

'Oh.' A surprised smile arrived, Corkbowl lifting his eyebrows. 'Oh, that's very nice, thanks.' He remembered Sunday's agenda. 'Sunday? Umm, Sunday's a problem because I've got to drive Esther to Kent as she's –'

'When do you have to set off?'

Corkbowl made a calculation. 'About three.'

'Then don't be such a prude, Corkbowl.' Beth drank her coffee. It didn't have the appeal of Corkbowl's flapjack. 'You'll have plenty of time.'

'Yes, I suppose,' said Corkbowl, the humble prude watching a hand stealing his food. 'If you're positive, as long as you're positive. I don't want you to go to any trouble for me.'

'You're no trouble.' Beth crossed her arms in confession. 'No, if anyone's trouble it'll be that Esther Hammerhans.' She shook her head, bothered. 'She's a nightmare; always eating everything politely, always complimenting the chef, always offering to wash up.'

Sarcasm didn't always translate to Corkbowl. He gave Beth an apprehensive look, a very mild one. It was the look of sniffing fresh milk and then not being sure. It made her laugh as she forced in the end of the flapjack. She talked with a palm over her stuffed mouth. 'Corkbowl!' She worked most of it down. 'I'm kidding.'

'So –' Corkbowl tried to appear blithe – 'Esther's coming to lunch, too?'

'Which is why it's a flawless plan. You'll both come to lunch and then leave for Kent together.'

'Yes,' said Corkbowl. 'Yes, that's true.' A hand took off his spectacles and rubbed an eye. Without the glasses his face was intriguing and changed. The glasses were returned and his face became familiar. 'Well, thank you very much, Beth.'

'And of course this invitation does extend to two if necessary,' said Beth, the great performer.

'Two?' Now Corkbowl understood. 'Ah, no, it's just me I'm afraid.'

'No girlfriend, Corkbowl?' Beth made a show of being astonished.

'Not at the moment. My last girlfriend was a while ago.' He counted back the months. 'Yes, quite a while ago.' To clarify just how distant that period was, Corkbowl added, 'I had a beard at the time.'

'Those must have been heady days,' said Beth, 'a beard *and* a girl-friend! Did you lose them simultaneously?'

'No,' Corkbowl smiled. A little laugh. 'No, the beard stayed around for a few weeks afterwards. The girlfriend left when she realized I didn't feel quite as serious about our relationship as she did. The beard left when I eventually realized it made me look like an animal that didn't care if it survived the winter.'

Beth was picturing this as he shyly dismissed a suggestion and then reconsidered. 'I could make something for lunch, if you like. If it would help. I'll cook a dish and bring it to your, ah . . .'

Beth had a range of excited questions.

'I've got a cod recipe. I bake it in foil.' He admitted confidently, 'I suppose it's my speciality.' The confidence dented. 'But the last time I made it, it was watery, so . . .' He remembered, curious. 'The flavour had rinsed away, for some reason.'

Beth offered a name. 'Rinsed cod.'

'Although . . .' Corkbowl pulled down an abacus thumb, tallying the possibilities. 'Although it might not be watery if I bake two smaller cod.' Yes, this was a plausible solution. 'I think if I use small young cod, then –'

'Suckling cod.'

'H'm?' Corkbowl committed it to memory. 'Suckling cod?'

'Yep, when they're fresh from their mothers. Or maybe it's when they're still with their mothers.' Beth nodded at him, liking his academic frown as he made hopeful adjustments to his recipe, liking his concentration at her jackass comments.

Corkbowl said, perky, 'And I've just bought a new jacket, so it would be a good opportunity to test it.' He suddenly got the joke. 'Still with their mothers!'

Beth leant on an elbow. 'Getting all dolled up in a new jacket, Corkbowl? I am flattered.'

'I wouldn't go that far, the jacket isn't exactly sensational.' Corkbowl made a joke of his own, 'Dulled up is probably the best I can manage.'

The cardigan dropped from Beth's shoulder as she stood. She caught it with a flamboyant mid-air snatch. 'Then you'll fit right in.'

26

Churchill was in his studio, sitting in the recess below the skylight. He was looking at a portrait of his father. His father, that obelisk in his life, was painted with a spotted bow tie partially concealed beneath a heavy fur coat, the fine points of his moustache teased into curling hooks. Churchill hadn't painted it; the painter was unknown. Once he had attempted to copy the portrait and had hallucinated, hearing his father speaking to him. It didn't speak now, although he wouldn't have minded if it did. Anything the painting said would be preferable to listening to the dog, positioned like a black hole in front of the window, blocking the light, chatting in his low, horrible voice.

Churchill stared venomously at the black hole. 'Can't you move?'

Black Pat slow-walked to a new position at the studio door, left open to let in the fertile scent of the orchard. Churchill strained round in his armchair to see where the dog had gone. The wooden armchair had been a gift from his friend Sir Ian Hamilton, its three stocky legs curving gracefully, spiralling rungs supporting the curved back-rest. A rag used for wiping paintbrushes in his hand, Churchill observed Black Pat.

Black Pat wasn't doing much, just sitting there tilting his nostrils at the ingredients in the breeze. But his presence made it difficult for Churchill to do any more work to his uncompleted painting of a pond with large golden orfe. He took the top off a tube of yellow paint and squeezed too hard. Paint coiled on to the palette in a high twisting mound.

Hanging above the studio door was another gift, a stuffed black bull's head, its giant neck attached to a wooden plaque. The plaque read: From one great warrior to another. The bull was a brave and fierce fighting bull slain by Manolete, a great Spanish matador. Churchill willed the bull, with his impressive horns, to pull from the moorings, fall, and gore the dog beneath. Nothing happened. Black Pat licked his jaws, making an infuriating wet sound.

Churchill assessed the goldfish painting again, finding nothing in it to be pleased with, and considered taking it across a knee and breaking it in half. His inspiration had wasted to cinders. He checked his watch and saw it was a good time to admit defeat. Clementine could be persuaded to have tea with him, or perhaps a glass of something more invigorating. He stood and took up his walking stick, the handle a carving of a bearded man's head, then made his way back through the orchard, following the trail flanked with flower beds. The trail joined a path running alongside a high yew hedge cut into turrets. The stone slabs of the path led to the terrace lawn and sloped up to the house. Churchill walked alone, Black Pat cantering ahead and letting himself into the house through the French doors of the dining room, negligently leaving the doors hanging open.

'Mrs Pussycat? Are you in here?'

She wasn't. Churchill went to Clementine's sitting room, a small, neat room near the main entrance at the front of the house.

'Clemmie?' There was no answer. 'Foul luck,' he muttered, re-routing to the drawing room.

At the sound of his steps Black Pat's face appeared, the huge mouth open in a slash of red. He was lying across a sofa, covering it. There were two in the room, on either side of the great marble fireplace, and Black Pat's bulk was clearly visible over the sofa's back.

Churchill let out a gruff *'Muh,'* and carried on moving, already halfway out of the room and into the hallway.

Leaping up, pastel cushions hitting the floor, Black Pat loped after him. They walked along together. Churchill looked at the top of the dog's massive skull and let himself flood with dusky sentiments, feeling Black Pat's dark magnetism drawing them out. Black Pat sensed Churchill's eyes and threw his face back, tongue slung down one cheek.

'Get away from me, you scapegrace,' Churchill said.

Black Pat said, 'I know where she is.'

Churchill told him, 'Our time together is a tourniquet of wire round my head, but it never leaves me so mentally destitute that I would allow myself to be led by you.'

Black Pat shook his ear at a grass seed buried in it, the wooden floor webbed with a pattern of drool.

'Clemmie?' Churchill shouted into another room, the library, feet and paws stifled on the Persian carpet.

'It won't give you any relief, talking to her,' said Black Pat, shuffling into Churchill's path, Churchill knocking against him. The dog stayed there, a hot muscular wall blocking Churchill's retreat. 'You should talk to me.'

'I don't want to hear your blimpish opinion,' Churchill said, swerving past and heading back out into the hall. He called hopefully, 'Clemmie?'

'Yes, Mr Pug?' Clementine's voice called back from upstairs. 'In here . . . I'm writing some letters. Do you want to come in with me and read for a while?'

He went up the stairs, the dog barging up next to him. Clementine was waiting in the doorway of her bedroom. The sunlight warmed the duck-egg blue walls and high barrel-vaulted ceiling, making them fluorescent. White roses radiated from a crystal vase on her writing desk. Before Black Pat could enter Churchill banged shut the door.

'I'll be here when you come out,' Black Pat hissed through the crack between the door and the floor.

'So wait, you bastard,' he heard Churchill mutter.

Black Pat crushed his snout so hard against the gap it bent to one side. 'I can wait for you in a way you can't comprehend. The days flash past like the rotating beam of a lighthouse and I wait through them. I will take what I have come for.'

Churchill reappeared at the door. Escaping to Clementine had shored up his heart. 'Oh, really. Well, what smokes cigars and doesn't give a fat damn?' Hammering the point squarely home, he retrieved a cigar from his breast pocket, lifted it to his mouth, and champed it. With a grin like a sunset he disappeared back behind the door to his wife.

'I was leaving anyway,' Black Pat called after him, and left.

27

8.30 p.m.

Esther was in the unused boxroom, unused much by anyone – either herself the house owner, or Black Pat the official lodger. She doodled with one of Michael's pencils. Shading with the pencil made a methodical sketching noise. An ornamental sword, drawn on graph paper, was improved by a pair of dolphins jumping over it. The dolphins were drawn with the word *'dolphin'* on their sides because they looked like thick snakes. Then she remembered dorsal fins. These were added. Back to the ornamental sword. Perhaps draft an eagle's foot making the A-OK sign next to this bit. Perhaps draft a pair of Corkbowl's spectacles there in honour of him being kind about having to drive her to Kent, in honour of him being kind and also quite handsome. It was a while before she realized Black Pat was watching her from the doorway.

'When did you get back?'

'Why, did you miss me?' Black Pat sat there, his shoulder against the wall. Not especially interested, Esther continued drawing. Black Pat hummed out a few seconds and heaved off, loitering over to her, dried leaves and muck scattering from his fur. He bulldozed to the space beside the desk. An unreasonable amount of slathering and grunting proved distracting, Black Pat lowering himself into a sphinx position on the worn carpet. Esther's pencil stopped, about to object, when she caught his expression. Initially buried anticipation, he replaced it with the expression of mindless contentment.

That space there, Black Pat there. It sparked a realization. Very fractured, Esther felt a shot of recognition, something distant coming closer in a drifting rainbow of greys. And it was lost as Black Pat said, 'Yikes.'

'What?'

'When you pull that face you look a hundred years old.'

She said drily, 'Thank you.'

Here came the clubbing of his hairy deadweight tail.

'Beth's invited me to lunch on Sunday.'

His tail went quiet. 'Sounds nice.'

'I suppose, I don't know. It's supposed to be nice.'

'Are you going?' A little twist in his tone wasn't keen.

As an experiment Esther tried to break the pencil in half with her thumb. It resisted. She ground her thumb against its ridged sides until the thumb hurt. This failed and she tossed the pencil so it rattled across the desk. 'It's difficult.'

'Difficult?' The twist had vanished, Black Pat pleased. 'Eating lunch?' He found an elastic band and ate it in a demonstration of the simplicity of eating. The rubber band escaped and he pounced after it, his chest catching the desk with a thwack. The band recaptured, he sank to his stomach, tearing up puckers of carpet. Privately his snout journeyed under Esther's chair to sniff her sock.

Esther's legs stretched out under the desk, the sock going with them. She put a hand on her stomach and rubbed it. 'It's hard to describe, I feel like I'm being cornered, like I'm –'

'Like you're lying in a crate full of meat?' This was delicious to Black Pat, the ultimate happiness.

'That's really repulsive,' said Esther. The lying analogy was useful though. Yes, it was a feeling of being laid down and waiting, of being held down. 'I do feel like I'm lying –'

'We're all lying in the gutter.' Black Pat's snout bashed the chair as he snatched it out, quick to interrupt. 'But, as the line goes, some of us have our heads in the road.'

'That isn't the line. It goes, but some of us are looking –'

'But some of us are looking at all the other idiots in the gutter, making plans . . .'

Esther scoffed at how infuriating he was. 'But some of us are looking at the *stars*.'

Black Pat misheard intentionally. 'Yes, some of us are looking at the cars, at all those cars. And wanting to lie in the comfortable cars.'

Esther rolled her head in a way that said: I give up. She said it. 'I give up.'

There was a quiet period. Esther's silence was withdrawn. Black Pat's silence became suspicious. She looked at him. He was sprawled on his side, nearly on his back, a slightly gratuitous pose. He was staring at the photograph replaced on the wall.

Esther found the intensity of his stare odd. It had an unusual quality, the picture transmitting a secret to him and causing a litmus-paper response that coloured through his wolfish features.

It wasn't exactly accusing, not dissimilar though, as he said, 'Why did you put it back up?'

'It's our wedding day.' This sounded like an excuse. 'It hung there before Michael moved it, so . . .' She let this trail off, mostly because the ending eluded her. The next sentence was a test. 'We were happier on that day than anyone has ever been.'

Impossibly cruel, Black Pat repeated it. 'Happier than anyone has ever been.'

A spined and poisonous thing was allowed to pass. Esther studied the photograph.

' . . . Both of you?'

'Yes.' She couldn't be certain.

Black Pat's following silence was an admission. Esther read it.

'You do know that Michael isn't living here any more.'

Black Pat made a noise in his throat, an oral nod.

'And do you know why?'

There was no answer.

Esther said, 'I think you do.'

No answer.

'I can't explain it.'

'So don't, Esther.'

A couple of seconds, and she said to him, ' . . . I think you're involved somehow.'

Black Pat lay there on the floor. 'That photograph, do you ever wonder why he took it down?'

Now it was Esther who didn't answer.

A crack of joints: the dog hauled on to his haunches. He put his head on the desk, inches from her. Esther sat stiff in her chair, alarmed by his strange intimacy.

At this short distance Black Pat's fur was revealed as several textures. The ruff of his neck fell in thick chunks, a downy insulating layer beneath. The pet-like fur on his head was fine and smooth. They stayed this way, the two of them. Then Black Pat turned down his mouth, a friendly thing. He wagged his head on the desk and was harmless. Esther's right hand touched the flat expanse between his ears. Her hand was tiny there, a pale object on the black barrel of his head. The shape of his skull was not as she imagined, its domed contours examined. Sick with apathy, Esther stroked the fur and said, 'I hate that you won't tell me how you're involved and what you know. And more than that, I hate that you can find it funny.'

'What?'

'You're always making jokes, you find it funny.'

'Oh, Esther.' He sounded tired. 'I don't find it funny.'

'No?'

'No.' Black Pat's head rolled to manoeuvre her hand to the base of his ecstatic ear. She scratched it, swearing never to eat with this hand again. Fur worked loose in clouds.

126

'Why don't you ask me what I know if it's that important?' He dared her. 'Go on, ask me.'

'Maybe I will.'

'Why not now?'

'Because . . .' She grinned in defeat. 'Because I don't want to know.' Her hand went to her lap. Black Pat made his ears tall in protest.

Esther had a question. 'So wait, if neither of us finds it funny, why do you make jokes?'

His eyebrow buds hitched, the connoisseur. 'Because we need the laughs.'

Saturday 25 July 1964

28

'There we go,' said Clementine, helping Churchill on with his navy blue jacket. She stood back. 'You look grand.'

Standing in the drawing room next to the east-facing window, Churchill stared down at himself. Behind Clementine, the dog, who had recently arrived, was leering at him. Black Pat raised a paw, Caesar style, and swung it round to the floor.

Churchill ignored him, turning to one of the large mirrors which hung at either side of the window. 'I look old,' he said to his reflection. 'I look like an old man.'

Black Pat's reflection nodded slowly behind him.

Clementine tutted, brushing Churchill's shoulders. 'Stop that. Here . . .' she folded a spotted silk handkerchief into his top pocket. 'That's for luck. You remember Marigold used to like this one?'

'Yes.' Churchill touched the handkerchief, remembering his dear young daughter who had died in 1921, before she was three. 'I miss her still, I miss our Duckadilly.'

Clementine's expression was kind. 'I know you do. I miss her terribly.' She went to a bunch of freshly cut flowers on the chimneypiece and busied herself, arranging them in a small vase. A bunch of oxeye daisies was laid nearby, intended for Churchill's bedroom.

Below the mirror a walnut side-table inlaid with medallions of satinwood held a silver-framed photograph of Diana, Churchill's oldest daughter, who had committed suicide the year before. She was standing with him on the porch of the Governor's house in the

Bahamas, a diminutive figure next to her dark-suited father. Diana had an engaging face, her dark bobbed hair brushed to the side, a belted white dress blowing against her shins. Churchill held the photograph, thoughts of his daughters in a display of black fireworks across the landscape of his memory.

Lying against the wall like a row of military sandbags, the dog was motionless apart from the swell of his ribcage.

Churchill replaced the photograph gently. 'I think I'll go to my study, Clemmie, and wait for the car there.' Churchill's steady steps climbed the staircase. Black Pat rocked to his feet, padding after him.

In the study Churchill sat heavily, a cigar in his hand, and reached for the box of matches on his desk. Squatting next to him Black Pat pushed the box out of range, nudging it to the farthest corner. Churchill was forced to stand, snatching at it. Back in his chair, Churchill struck a match. A flame sprang up. Held steady between teeth, the cigar went to meet it. The tobacco didn't catch. Black Pat's wet tongue shot out, smothering the flame. It was obscene.

'Stop it.'

Churchill looked at the dog. His tongue had reeled out like a grey vine.

'I'm warning you. *Desist*,' Churchill said to him in a challenge.

Black Pat grinned, face pleating, watching as Churchill puffed at the cigar.

'I can only presume you'll be accompanying me to this press conference.' Churchill's fingers dragged across his forehead from the temples and met.

Black Pat put his chin on the desk, papers crumpling beneath it. 'Of course. We've had it arranged for decades, haven't we?'

Churchill stared out of the window at the green slopes below. On the wall above the fireplace was a huge painting of Blenheim Palace, the place in which he had unintentionally been born – his mother going into labour early while visiting relatives. 'I've wondered on occasion whether you were there, waiting to stake your flag from the moment my soul entered this world.'

'I didn't come until sent for.' Black Pat's eyes were like leeches on him. 'But I've been a companion to others around you, so I've never been far away.'

Churchill heard in this answer references to his father, his daughter Diana, other family members rising and disintegrating.

Clementine had finished arranging the vase of daisies on his bedroom windowsill. Her voice called through from the landing. 'So when will you be back, Winston?'

Churchill turned away from Black Pat, brutalized. 'What you've done, the damage you've done . . .' His tone was windswept. ' . . . The node of your corrosive presence in our family tree, it is at times more than I can endure.'

'Mr Pug?' called Clementine, coming to the study. 'When do you think you'll be back?'

'Oh, I don't know, not long I hope,' Churchill answered. 'Those hacks will no doubt want to grill me interminably.'

Clementine was at the doorway, a hand on the frame. 'Don't give them a hard time, Mr Pug. They're only doing their job.'

'I know, I know.' Churchill took a pull on his cigar and exhaled a funnel of smoke. 'But they are all such boobs.'

At the sound of wheels crawling across gravel Clementine went to the window, looking down on to the drive at the front of the house. 'Your car is here.'

'Right-o,' said Churchill, getting up. 'See you soon, Clemmie.'

With a kiss he lumbered down the stairs. Black Pat went too, storming ahead. Paws hammering the steps, he hit the bottom with a clatter of claws on the black-tiled floor of the narrow hall.

The scene was watched with melancholy eyes by Rufus the poodle. He curled round the dried pig's ear in his bed and hid his face.

Clementine came downstairs as Churchill closed the car door, the car easing in an arc away from the house, then moving faster, its engine becoming faint as it set off on the hour's drive to Westminster. Clementine looked at the poodle. 'I know, Roofy,' she said to him. 'I know exactly what you mean.'

29

The streaming activity was gone at the weekends, Westminster Palace now serene and ornamental with deserted corridors. Corkbowl was enjoying it, feeling like a Robinson Crusoe type among the unexplored shelves. The reason for him being there, a thick book of British road maps, had been located and discarded in favour of one about Morocco. The pictures were of an exotic fantasy world, bustling souks, stalls with baskets full of spices and piles of woven cloth, people pouring through the thin pathways between. Corkbowl would get to road maps immediately after just a quick look at this other book detailing the history of the Tower of London.

When Esther walked into the reference room, Corkbowl yanked round, not expecting to see anyone. His dark hair was more spirited at weekends, Corkbowl not bothering to subdue it. He hadn't shaved and it suited him. Shirtsleeves folded to the elbow, he walked from behind the table. Esther saw his trousers were tucked into his socks.

Corkbowl noticed at the same time. 'Yep. I know what you're thinking, how debonair.'

She smiled as he said, 'And you're probably also thinking that it's a very adventurous look for a Saturday morning, very Courrèges.'

'I am now. Although Courrèges is more futuristic, isn't he? You need to add a few metallic touches.'

'An aluminium jacket. Got you.' Deep lines appeared down his cheeks when he grinned, as he did at the idea of an aluminium jacket.

'And that's even safer on the roads when I ride my bike.' He came clean. 'The socks are because I rode my bike, if I'm honest.'

'Thought so,' answered Esther. 'I had a suspicion.'

He relaxed, hands in his pockets. 'Do you often come to the library at the weekends?'

'Not usually, but I've not got a lot on . . . There wasn't much happening at home and I . . .' She felt a flush of embarrassment at this disclosure. 'I didn't finish my work the other day. It seemed a good chance to get it done. You know what the library can be like in the week . . .' The implication was that the library was an indulgence of lawless distractions.

She said it lightly but Corkbowl registered an undertone. She knew he had heard it, a nude and unashamed truth rolling there. Esther scrambled to think of something funny to say to disguise her loneliness. The spotlight shone on an empty stage.

It was Corkbowl who saved her. 'And we've got to go to Kent tomorrow. As your chaperone I thought I'd better take advantage of my access to all the maps they have in here so that I don't get us totally lost.'

A brilliant excuse. 'Exactly,' Esther said. 'If I'm going to meet Sir Winston Churchill, the least I should do is practise my typing.'

'Which is also why I've taken my car to be serviced. It's an old car and I want to make sure it behaves.' Corkbowl bowed gallantly. 'No flames under the bonnet this time, m'lady.' He checked his wristwatch. 'I've got to cycle over and fetch it in half an hour, so I'm not here for long.'

'Oh, right,' Esther said. 'Yes, awful,' she said, carefully airy, 'work on a Saturday! I'm going to get out as soon as possible.'

'It could be more awful, though,' Corkbowl said, not finding it awful at all, 'Dennis-John could be here too.' He scanned around the room, checking. 'In fact, I'm sort of surprised he isn't. I can't imagine anywhere else would let him in.'

'I think his wife lets him into the house sporadically to terrorize their two children.'

'His wife?' A stunned Corkbowl. 'He's got children?'

'And a tortoise.' Esther added, 'I suppose because Dennis-John can't bite through the shell.'

'Dennis-John the family man?' Corkbowl considered it. 'Quick, we'd better change the subject. If I think about this too hard my brain will need help getting in and out of the bath.'

She laughed and it made him wish they could stay here all day. But she was here now and it was not an opportunity to be missed. Corkbowl pointed to a thermos flask standing on a table. 'Do you fancy joining me for a drink?' He tempted her with some flask facts. 'The thermos comes with its own plastic mug and I washed it this morning.' A final temptation followed, Corkbowl showing off the socks still over his trousers: 'Esther, don't pretend you can resist these legs.'

They sat at a table. Corkbowl twisted off the mug and filled it with tea for her. It was now that Corkbowl realized there was only one mug between them.

'Do you mind if I . . .' He lifted the thermos to his lips, prepared to drink directly from the neck.

Through a sip she urged him, one hand swiping in a gesture of consent.

'Actually, wait,' said Corkbowl. 'We can't let an occasion like this go by without a few library-inspired words.' He cleared his throat, as if addressing thousands. 'To nearly quote Groucho Marx, outside of a thermos a book is a man's best friend . . .' Corkbowl took a huge grinning swig, too much of a grin for drinking. He cleaned his chin with a quick cuff. ' . . . And inside a thermos it's too dark to read.' The flask lifted in an affectionate salute.

'I'll drink to that.' Esther held her cup out to toast the flask.

Gentle wind drifted in through the open window and carried the scent of baked tarmac and the muddy kiss of the river. Latticed diamonds of glass lit yellow. A herring gull cried. A beautiful morning, a day for fish and chips on the beach.

Corkbowl said, 'So I've been invited to Beth's this Sunday. I think you're going too?'

'U'm-h'm.' Esther spoke into her mug.

A different atmosphere made her pause, gamma rays rolling through the pale neutrality of the library. The yellow windows had changed.

'Great,' Corkbowl answered. 'It should be fun.'

Heavy steps came up the centre of the room behind the partition. She waited. Then there he was. Black Pat crooked a cowboy elbow, propped against a bookcase.

Esther glanced at Corkbowl. Black Pat was easily visible, a few metres away and colossal. Corkbowl chatted, enjoying his flask. He turned his head reflexively to see what Esther was looking at, and turned back. Maybe he was talking about his car, Esther didn't hear. She readied herself for Corkbowl's reaction, ready for him to leap. He did the opposite, he put a hand behind his neck and scratched there; he put an ankle on a knee and then took it off.

Esther said cautiously to Corkbowl, her finger pointed at the bookcase, 'Can't you see –'

'He can't,' Black Pat interrupted. 'Here, I'll show you . . .'

Corkbowl was peering after Esther's finger. Black Pat bopped about at the bookcases, making a spooky noise. Esther watched as absolutely nothing happened on Corkbowl's face.

'See?' Black Pat said to Esther. 'I'm all yours.'

'Sorry, what were you pointing at?' Corkbowl asked.

'Say anything,' instructed Black Pat. Esther was distracted as he said, 'Say you saw a dragon fly.'

Esther obediently said, 'I saw a dragon.' Corkbowl's head inclined to the left, politely puzzled. 'A dragon fly,' said Esther.

'Crikey,' Corkbowl said with gracious interest.

Esther made a decision. She said to Corkbowl suddenly, 'This might be a mistake, but do you mind if I tell you something, as an experiment . . .'

'Careful, Esther,' Black Pat said. 'Lives are built on the foundations of three little words.'

A vicious trick. Esther remembered Michael saying these three little words.

'An experiment?' Corkbowl adjusted his spectacles, ready to be of assistance. 'What did you want to tell me?'

'Three little words,' said Black Pat. '*Trial and error*. You have to take possession of those that are yours.' He repeated, 'And I'm all yours, Esther.'

'Esther?' Corkbowl said to her. 'Are you okay?'

'Who is this Pinocchio?' Black Pat's voice was jealous. 'Why are you talking to such a weird Pinocchio?'

Corkbowl had an innocent expression when serious and concentrating, his face like the sweet face on the underside of a stingray. It gave her courage. 'Actually,' she admitted, 'I wouldn't say I'm completely okay.'

'Esther –' Black Pat made a drawstring motion with his claws – 'zip it.'

Corkbowl said softly, 'Is there something I could perhaps help you with . . .'

Perhaps he could. 'Two years ago,' Esther was speaking fast, 'I was married . . .'

'You're married?' Corkbowl hid his disappointment.

'Not any more, no.'

'Tut tut.' Black Pat bumped down on to four feet. He pawed his way forwards.

'I was married to a man called Michael.'

On his giant haunches he was next to her. A cold and nasty sensation, Black Pat's nose touched her temple. 'You can't sell Michael's dignity to this goose.'

Corkbowl's arm created a minor emergency, knocking the flask. He bent to delve for a handkerchief in his pocket.

Esther hushed Black Pat. 'I wouldn't be betraying Michael.'

Black Pat's mouth was in a fat grin. 'Those are your words, not mine. Betrayed is your word, Esther.'

Corkbowl doubled his handkerchief over and kept mopping. This action worked round his wristwatch and he saw the time.

Black Pat wore his grin, lavishly fat. '*Checkmate.*'

The garage. Corkbowl had to go, already five minutes late for his car. Apologizing, his socked shins carried him in long strides. At the doorway he was compelled back.

'Before I leave . . . I wanted you to know that if there is anything I can do . . .' The sentence finished there. He banged the wall with the mallet of his fist, trumped. Then an idea.

Corkbowl's emotional side was a weak speaker, but his general knowledge side could occasionally translate.

'I've been reading about volcanic eruptions and it occurred to me that there are some, ah . . . There might be metaphorical correlations with other . . .' He realized he must appear magnificently obscure, and he was babbling. What was wrong with his stupid mouth? He took his sensibilities by the throat. 'To survive a volcano eruption you analyse the lava flow. If it streams to the left or right, you're out of danger. It's if the lava appears still that you're in real jeopardy.'

Esther was listening. Also listening was Black Pat. He had on an expression of such pioneering sarcasm it forced a double chin.

Corkbowl continued: 'Because that means that it's coming straight at you, and you should run for your life.'

'Right,' said Esther.

'*Balls*,' said Black Pat.

Corkbowl moved his head in a bartering gesture. 'Of course that's assuming you've survived the initial magma missiles flung high into the air.'

'Let's definitely assume that.' Maybe she understood? She thought so.

Corkbowl gave her a smile. 'I appreciate it's not your typical offer, but I just wanted to mention it in case you ever need a volcanologist, I suppose.'

30

With Corkbowl gone, Black Pat lolled about in the reference room, basking in Esther's complaints. Alone with her he relaxed. She tried to ignore him as he padded her with one of his paws.

A new tactic to punish him was writing notes on a pad and acting highly engrossed. Black Pat clowned for attention. His claws caught the carpet weave, dragging him in inches. Esther didn't look at him, except when she accidentally did. He tossed on his back and cycled his legs. Now flipped to his stomach, he put his doleful snout on the floor, sad to be ignored. 'You really wanted to talk to that goose Corkbowl?'

'I might have done, yes.' Esther swizzled the pen in her mouth. 'Possibly.' A coy attempt to justify it followed. 'I don't know, he seems so . . .' She said the last word too quietly.

'Digestible?' Black Pat volunteered.

'Likeable.'

She was thinking of Corkbowl and he watched her, sensing that a little seed of warmth had taken root and needed to be usurped. The ugliness of his mood surprised her.

'Your trust in Corkbowl cheapens you. And it cheapens Michael. Confiding in him is a mistake you will learn to regret.'

'Wait, I haven't –'

Black Pat said, 'But you considered it, Esther.'

Esther juggled for an explanation. She gave up. 'It doesn't matter, I'm glad I didn't tell him.' She frowned, certain. 'Yes, I'm glad.'

'So am I.' A yap of exertion carried Black Pat to his feet, now cheery again. He swung to Esther's side. Beside his mastodon bulk her head was at an ideal height. A chin-rest. He tested it out. The furry chin drove her into a hunch as it bore down. Both hands fought him away. Esther smoothed the halo of her static hair. She told Black Pat that he had changed everything for the worse.

'I haven't changed anything. I may have provided some . . .' he made a seasoning motion with a paw, sprinkling it, ' . . . variety.'

'I'd rather you hadn't.'

'Nonsense,' he said. 'Variety is the spice of life.' No, he could do better. 'Wait, variety is the *ice* of life.' Out came a satisfied smirk. 'It's *cool*.'

Esther scrubbed an eyelid. 'You're so frustrating.' She picked up her pen. 'I've barely got the energy to do this.' The pen was thrown at him.

A snack, Black Pat's mouth caught the pen and shattered the plastic. The ink flowed over his tongue and was a delicious sauce. He spoke again and his tongue was blue. 'Variety,' he said, this thing he was about to say delighting him, 'is the *dice* of life. You win some, you lose some.' He sent a look over his shoulder. 'You win some and you lose some. But, Esther, it's a game you have to play.'

'You play it, then.'

'I am,' he instantly replied.

She preferred to disregard it, preferring instead to continue with the notes. She immediately missed her eaten pen. Esther cast a silent indecent curse at the lost pen, at Black Pat.

A purposeful noise came from behind her and made her turn, curious. Black Pat's concentration was intense, his posture now alert. With the stance of a working Alsatian, he received instruction.

'Black Pat?'

He pounded to the doorway, to the corridor. Esther called him and it caused a fleeting head shift and then indifference. This corridor would take him upstairs to the Royal Gallery.

143

'Where are you going?'

From upstairs came the summons. Black Pat was motionless, the silhouette of his body stiff-braced. Esther was forgotten and he broke into a hunting run.

31

The high ceilings had swimming-pool acoustics and resonated with conversation. Huge muddy paintings of battles covered the red and gold walls. This was the Royal Gallery, a grand chamber in the hive of Westminster Palace. It was filled with journalists from national and regional newspapers. Westminster Palace on a Saturday! The novelty of it created an ambience of bonhomie. The journalists joshed around, gossiping. Then conversation stopped, heads bending to the entrance.

A swish of bodies drew back to create a path. The dark tugboat of Churchill cruised through to a table at the head of the room. He was joined by his friend and MP for Shrewsbury, Sir John Langford-Holt. At the table Langford-Holt coughed self-consciously into his palm, alerting the journalists. Churchill took a seat and scanned his notes, elbows resting on the papers.

The journalists craned nearer, staring at Churchill's bowed head. They stared at his pink crown. He looked up from his notes and monitored them sternly.

'Good afternoon, gentlemen,' said Langford-Holt. 'Welcome to Westminster. We are glad you could accommodate our slightly irregular schedule and attend this Saturday afternoon. As most of you know, today's gathering is to announce that our esteemed ex-Prime Minister and MP for Woodford, Sir Winston Churchill, will be retiring from parliament on Monday the twenty-seventh of July. Naturally press will be covering that date, but we wanted to provide this smaller event, as an opportunity to ask Sir Winston a few questions about his career before the more general affair of the twenty-seventh.'

There was a racing of pens on paper. Hands bolted into the air, ripe with questions. One of the journalists was invited to relay his enquiry.

He introduced himself. 'Mr David Fallow from *The Times*, sir. Sir Winston, could you tell us how you feel about coming to the end of your illustrious career?'

Churchill said, 'I feel honoured to have been a part of the history of this great country and will remember my time in government with deep pride. I hope that I have served the people of Britain well.'

Another journalist was selected. 'What will you do with your time on leaving?'

Churchill joked, 'Delight my wife with my unabated company, whether she likes it or not.' There was laughter and Churchill smiled. 'Clementine's pretty quick on her feet, let me tell you, gentlemen. But I always track her down. And, as well as catching up with her, I also hope to catch up with my painting and reading.'

'What will you be reading, sir?'

'Hopefully the labels on vintage wine and menus in good restaurants.'

More laughter filled the room. A hand was chosen from the crop of raised arms.

'Is there anything you regret?'

Churchill thought briefly. 'Oh, I don't know. I think so. Isn't there always? We make the choices we can with the information available to us at the time. I take solace in the knowledge that I always made the decision I felt right, and did it for noble reasons with the consequences in mind. But the passage of events will confound even the best-laid plans. I suppose this is what we all learn in life. I have certainly learnt this lesson well.'

'Mr Jacob McKeith of the *Evening Standard*, sir. What do you feel has been your most valuable lesson learnt over the years?'

Churchill answered firmly. 'There have been many. One is courage. Courage is rightly esteemed the first of human qualities because it is the quality which guarantees all others. I have also learnt love, and would say that my most brilliant achievement was my ability to persuade Clementine Hozier to marry me. She is my polestar and has been a source of exceptional strength for me throughout the years.'

Another question was sanctioned. 'Is there anything you still want to do?'

'Vast amounts,' said Churchill. 'I wouldn't mind visiting 44 Avenue de Champagne, the world's most drinkable address. This, the Pol Rogers' chateau in Epernay, is the maker of my favourite brand of champagne. It's no secret that I wouldn't mind a couple of sun-filled days over there, sampling a few bottles, treading the grapes with my feet.'

The journalists visualized this.

Churchill added, 'Don't worry, gentlemen. I'll make sure those specific Churchill-pressed bottles don't go into circulation.'

'What else do you enjoy?' asked a journalist.

'A great many things. Along with a glass of Pol Roger, a cigar is always welcome, namely Romeo y Julieta. That's a premium smoke, a cigar of great craftsmanship.'

All journalists knew this. They wrote it down anyway. At the back of the room behind them a black totem rose from the floor. No big fan of press conferences, Black Pat had been dozing against the wall. Now he was on his feet. Churchill watched the dog indirectly, letting his peripheral vision monitor the massive head hanging above the unaware audience. A bad sign. Usually he stayed lying in the corridors outside like a shot elephant, totally uninterested.

A journalist with flat blond hair asked, 'So, Sir Winston, with all

147

your interests and hobbies, especially after such a long and peri-odically testing political career, it sounds as though you are thoroughly looking forward to Monday's retirement. At your age it must be quite a relief to have the prospect of, ah, uncomplicated diversions.'

Churchill exhaled. 'Uncomplicated?' He dropped back, pushed into the chair. 'I should dearly . . .' Over his face passed a shadow of discomposure. The lusting Black Pat knew what was coming.

'There are two answers to your question,' Churchill said. 'The first is an uncomplicated text, full of easiness and simplicity. But study it and there are footnotes. And as footnotes do, they lead us to an original source, the source of influence. The second answer is in these footnotes, which bear witness to an alternate forecast.' When Churchill spoke again his tone was introspective. 'Gentlemen, may I suggest to you that the entitlement to immortality felt so noisily in youth is not always relinquished in our dotage. We are not all of us blessed in this way.' He looked at the blond man. 'At my age, as you put it to me . . . sir, I wish there was such a thing, for I find the internal self remains stoutly resistant to time's seasons.' His lips shrugged. 'Because here's the truth: while the mind is a tran-scendental pilgrim, the body is an animal. And this animal will carry you as far as it can. Glad of the burden, it will struggle on its knees to serve, fighting out the inches in dust and desert. But do never forget where it is migrating to, for it will bear you there. It is a migra-tion into the dusk.'

Churchill cast a glance at the dog. Still on his feet, Black Pat seemed fascinated.

Churchill addressed the journalists. 'So when you ask me if I look forward to retirement, for these reasons I cannot say I leap to it. I am driven to it and I have dug in my heels, let me tell you, because work is a holy distraction from these morbidities. Yet as retirement comes despite my efforts, I prepare for these approaching years with the reserve I would feel if I were dressing my neck with a gaboon viper as opposed to . . . say . . .' he thought of an opposite, '. . . being seated to dine on minute steak.'

The journalists were writing this down, feeling squeamishly aware of their animal bodies. A few checked their watches, brooding for the pub. The blond journalist would definitely never ask this question again.

Black Pat chomped his jaws in a small bark, the atmosphere a lullaby to him. Churchill crumpled a piece of paper in his fist. He toughed out a smile. The crowd of journalists turned back up at him, dreading it.

'Pah, aren't we the gang of whelps and jugginses. Forgive me. I didn't intend to waft in such a miasma of spiritual famine. Anyway –' he surveyed them, these men decades younger – 'you needn't much concern yourselves, you're all just ducklings.' Churchill smiled, this smile coming freely. 'Have gumption, my dear ducklings.'

Black Pat's tail lifted, wary of the change in Churchill's tone, then drooped at the next comment.

'And should you remember this fear, remember courage equally,' said Churchill. 'Beard the fear with courage.'

Beard the fear, wrote the journalists, some with question marks.

'For,' said Churchill, speaking to the faces and the canine face above, fastening his hard eyes on that canine face, 'you can't stop fear snaring you with a headstall, and you can't stop it landing a buss on your headstone, but you can damn well try.'

A long staid period, fiercely awkward. A hand lifted. No one welcomed it, desperate for the easy release of the pub.

'Yes, your question please,' said Langford-Holt

'Sir Winston.' The journalist cleared his throat. 'In 1929 you caught a one hundred and eighty-eight pound marlin.' He coached himself. Out came the ridiculous question: 'Do you have any fishing tips for readers?'

Muffled sarcastic laughter. Jackals near the stricken journalist made trumpeting sounds.

Langford-Holt gave him a brisk stare. 'Are you representing a legitimate newspaper?'

The journalist lifted his shoulders. 'I also freelance for a fishing journal. Thought I might . . .'

Churchill cut in. 'An excellent query. Yes, by God let's refresh the mood.' He grinned broadly as Black Pat huffed. Black Pat made a teenage flop with one arm, a thwarted move, absolutely bored. It was the move of a gambler flinging his tickets to the floor, hating his losing horse.

Churchill said, 'I'd advise your fishing readers who aspire to other than a brown trout that the waters of California are certainly a more glamorous affair.'

Relief spread through the room, even Langford-Holt slacking into his chair. The spectre of mortality lost its teeth, replaced by an unexpected interest in angling.

'And for those game readers who harbour a pash to land one of Neptune's giants, I'd urge them to make ready for battle,' said Churchill. The memory of that day in California was vivid, a triumph of sporting happiness. 'It was a dramatic experience, wrestling that marlin. We would meet, that much was certain, the marlin and I. The problem was on whose terms. I tried to haul him in, and he tried to haul me over, warring like a typhoon. I eventually drew him to me, raging and punching his head against the line. More than once he nearly succeeded in hurling me from the bow. Ho!' Churchill knocked down an amused fist. 'I would have gone off behind him like a bottle rocket.'

32

6.30 p.m.

Light made a pair of tennis shorts over the bedroom wall. A shirt dropped on the floor had developed a modest beauty, cultivating the painterly creases of a restaurant napkin. On the windowsill was a small balding plant. The magic of the late light made it gorgeous and exotic.

Esther stared from her bed, blind to these things. She lay on her side of the mattress. A hand explored the other side and it was a dictionary of loss. Up came the hand, disturbed by something disgusting. A tuft of collected fur. Over the bed, over everything, were long black hairs, a smell in the room. Black Pat had been in here? But he had been everywhere. Forget it, there were other things to think about. The bed made an angry twang. That was new. So he had crashed around on her bed and damaged the springs. She found the energy to work up a docile grunt.

A moment of decadent self-pity ensued. She wallowed. Then she quickly sat up.

'Y'ello?' It was Black Pat's voice from downstairs. Paws made a whacking ascent. Sniffs came at the stairhead and sucked at the edges of the bedroom door, the shiny bulb of his nose against the paintwork. 'Esther?'

'I'm reading.'

This was a tart and clear instruction to leave her alone. Shoving the door open, Black Pat burst through like a bowling ball smashing into fresh pins.

'Hello,' he said coolly, registering the scene on the bed. 'So you were reading, were you?'

An old but unread copy of *Moby Dick* lay peacefully by her knee, a bowl of oxidizing fruit salad on top. A bar of Dairy Milk was not completely eaten. Black Pat's eyes veered to the book, took a scornful holiday there, and then travelled back to hers.

'It must be a riveting read.'

'It's quite brilliant. At least that's what it says on the dust jacket.' Esther took off a block of chocolate with her teeth.

Black Pat was moving around her, now at the foot of the bed, obscuring the wardrobe. Now blocking the window.

'But I am about to read,' Esther said. She opened the book at random. 'Drink ye harpooners! Drink and swear . . .' This was recited aloud, proof of how absorbed she was in the text. 'So if you don't mind, I'd like to be left alone.'

Uncooperative, Black Pat's front legs went on the sheets, lingering for her objections. She did nothing, eating more chocolate and pretending to read. This was all she did, and it was therefore an act of compliance.

The hind legs bent to jump and jumped. Entirely on the bed, Black Pat was cartoonishly too large and heavy for it, furious twangs coming from the springs.

'Hey!' she cried in a shout. His trundling rotations trampled near her, driving great ruts in the mattress. '*Black Pat!*' she shouted again, and he didn't hear her over his nasal humming, a tune in the spirit of housework as he obeyed the canine instinct to circle. His paws caught in the quilt and dragged it up into a nest. He dug at the nest with his claws and there was the rip of laddering fabric. A mighty ricochet went through the structure of the injured bed as he hurled himself down with an animal rumble of comfort: *Mrrrt*.

Esther tried to push him to the floor and he retaliated by rolling on her arms. She rescued her arms and gave him a cross jab with her toe. The toe snatched away as his mouth came to challenge it.

Black Pat lifted his head. 'Your side is much more comfortable.'

His lifted head showed her a smiling profile. 'What's orange, purple, the colours of the four humours, a type of grey, and brown?'

'I don't know.' Esther waited. 'What is?'

Black Pat's paw made a flop in the area around her knees, a feeble shake.

Esther searched for the answer and couldn't find it. 'What is?' she said again. 'What's your stupid punchline?'

'That's the punchline. That fruit salad.' The paw joggled on its wrist in the direction of her bowl. 'It stinks.'

Ridiculous. Esther ignored him, finishing the bar of chocolate. Black Pat watched her, his stomach expressing itself with a sound of bubbling mud. Unmoved, she sat cross-legged on her tiny corner of the bed. Black Pat punished her selfishness by abusing the division of the mattress. Rudely he budged his way over. Her muscles were indignant at the pressure of his body. But she wouldn't be chased from her own room. All attempts to force him back only made him more enamoured of the game. The bowl was toppled and soaked the bed with juices. A grape escaped Esther's hurried efforts to clean up the spilled fruit. Interesting, a grape. Black Pat chewed it and then wiped his horrified tongue down the length of a foreleg. A short period of inactivity occurred and ended as he bulked his massive hips, knocking Esther. He said insincerely, 'Oops!'

Esther pleaded with the wall. 'Could you please get out of my room.'

'You get out. I can't.' Black Pat caught a hiccup in his throat and then made a foul frazzled rasp. His ear felt a fleck of something and performed a whip.

His eyes turned aside, she felt him studying her indirectly, studying her with his other senses. 'Black Pat, I can never understand what you're . . . Why do you always talk in riddles?'

Black Pat lay calmly. 'Riddle sticks.'

Esther was confused at his grannyish oath. ' . . . Fiddlesticks?'

'Riddle,' a sarcastic gap was inserted, 'sticks.'

'That's such rubbish.'

'*Fiddlesticks*,' Black Pat said with a wide grin. Then he thrust his neck on to Esther's pillow, which bunched by the headboard. He tested the durability of cotton with his jaws, feathers appearing at a new hole. Dirt from his paws made brown stripes on the sheets and bedding, his dirt and pungency turning the bed into a hideous place. He caressed the corner of her book with his mouth to analyse the texture. She swiped the book from him and felt pulp in her fingers.

'Black Pat! You've got the manners of an animal.'

A triumphant expression: 'I am an animal.'

Esther examined the ruined pages. 'You're supposed to be my lodger.'

'I think you recognize what I am.'

She looked from the book; Black Pat was watching her with the gaze of a predatory animal. He said, 'I am given my assignments and I follow them without deviation. Esther, you should recognize that I do not deviate in my residence here.' He said in a horrible coax, 'Come on, you know that.'

So she was part of his assignment. It was the crescendo of a piano heaved from the top of a staircase. The piano hit the floor and detonated with all chords. Yes, she supposed she had known. Why hadn't he told her this before?

'Because it was inappropriate.'

Esther perched on her small corner of the invaded bed, in her invaded house. She thought of Michael and those days. Thoughts swarmed in droves to the boxroom study. She closed her eyes to find Michael in her library. He appeared automatically, wolf-whistling at Big Oliver's new wellington boots. Another memory was selected, Michael with a messy smile, waking up in this bed and denying that he snored. Here he was standing in the front room, posing with a Christmas tree. Here he was, running away from her snowball and not getting far. The camera shutter went down and came up on Michael burning an omelette, lifting one end with a spatula and blaming the frying pan. The shutter went down and came up on Michael looking awestruck and kissing Beth at the hospital after Little Oliver was born. And there were the other times when he was sitting in exhausted solitude in his study. There he was sitting bent in the garden with his elbow on the bench. There he was – a deathly silence on him, binding him. These places where Michael had sat alone, Esther saw them. Yet not alone, for every minute of that time Black Pat had sat with him, his body wearing out a sandy trench in the garden, wearing the carpet by the desk into a patch.

'You were here in this house.'

'Not just here.'

Then where?

'In a lot of places, almost all of them.'

Something terrible flowered. 'Black Pat, did you make him do it?'

Black Pat fawned in his loathing of this question. 'No.'

'Were you with him?'

No answer. Low sunlight through the window, the sky lilac. It would go from lilac to indigo, from today to tomorrow. The room had the moist heat of compost.

'Black Pat, could you have stopped him?'

An answer of sorts: a paw coming closer and sorry.

'You didn't even try and stop him?'

'Esther,' Black Pat's words came pensively. 'I can't.'

'You mean you won't.'

'I mean I can't. Esther, you must understand what I am.'

Yes she knew what he was, she told him. No she didn't, he explained. Let me tell you, Esther.

'I'm only the grease in a crease,' he said. 'A kink in the link.'

What did that mean? His reply was complicated and elusive. It was useless. He was so meek: 'There's a reason why I'm a dog, with the

155

desires of a dog. If I could have resisted the compulsion and left Michael I would have lain in the grass like a bonnet monkey and searched for nits.' Black Pat became taken by the poetry of this fantasy. 'I would have picked for nits, a harmless nanny goat with a bell on her collar.' Out came a bellyaching moan. 'But I am not benign. I'm a dog with the hunger of a dog and I am compelled by it.'

He was desperate for her to understand: Listen, Esther, the strength of the compulsion is terrifying; a violent and depthless appetite. It's a lust from a cosmology of carnivorous instincts, all those instincts channelled into one incinerating white-hot heart streaming with smoke and magnesium.

Esther listened. She pulled a loose thread on her top. She listened to Black Pat, letting him explain without interruption. 'So you see,' he said, 'I don't have a choice.'

Was Michael given a choice? No. It wasn't a matter of choice. Black Pat spoke of the photograph in the drawer. Look at it, Esther. Look at it again, take it from the nail and pore over it.

Off the bed like a hawk and into the boxroom, the photograph in her hands. Their wedding day, hers and Michael's. She scrutinized the familiar landmarks: the wedding guests, her head back in laughter, Michael turning to smile at someone. Petals of confetti. The car door open to show a bottle of champagne. Behind them the church. Flagstones and rose bushes; a committee of stones in the graveyard. Esther searched the photograph. All was the same. She kept searching. And she found it.

The car door was open and the window mirrored the church. Wedding guests applauded, gloved hands clapping, a baby in a white cap. But there behind them in the window of the car, in the mirrored image of the church steps. A shape captured amidst the distractions of flapping dresses and corsages. Just visible, just a small irregularity in the reflection.

His ears were in lax salute, two black tips. The reflection captured the curve of his bullish shoulders. Too small in the mirroring window, his features were lost. The angle of his head gave away his attitude: a relaxed ownership, watching Michael and covetous. An observer at this event, Black Pat set himself away on the steps: You can go, Michael. But back you'll come. Off you go, but not for long. Back you'll come because I'll bring you back.

'I met him a long time before you did. He took the photograph down towards the end because he didn't want to be reminded of this. It got worse.' Black Pat had followed her to the boxroom. Sulking with guilt, he looked for a distraction. Good friends with the corner of the desk, he gave it a gnawing.

Esther shoved his head from the desk. 'Why didn't Michael tell me about you?'

Black Pat was on the worn patch of carpet by the desk. 'Why haven't you told anyone about me?'

She sat on the edge of the desk and floundered for a reply. 'How can I?' She asked him genuinely, 'How could I begin to talk about you? When I tell myself it sounds impossible, and that's with you sitting opposite me.' She said, stumped, 'I thought about telling Corkbowl, and then I realized that even if I did he wouldn't know how to believe me, would he? It's absurd.'

'Absurd, yes,' said Black Pat, 'totally absurd!' He had sunk to the floor.

Esther thought about Michael in here with this dog, trapped with him, already trapped when they first met. 'And you're going to trap me too.' She recalled the day he moved in, her gullibility. 'This is an ambush.'

'No, it's an affinity. I didn't initiate it.' From behind the desk Black Pat said, 'The magnet that keeps me here is the magnet which brought me here. We are twinned by the same orbit and I'm all yours. Esther, I'm all yours.' He said hopefully, 'Don't you like me even slightly?'

'I –' Esther was smothered by a weight of contempt, hating herself because she hated her answer. 'I suppose I do. I suppose I don't really have an option.'

His answer was a version of the truth. 'You don't. We have an affinity and it chains us.' He wanted to soothe her though. 'Cosy chains,' he said, willing her to be soothed, to be resigned.

Esther shut her eyes. Her response to this was no response. But it wasn't entirely the lapse into resignation he had wanted, a glimmer of defiance remaining beneath.

Black Pat's face came up above the desk, just half of it, the top of his big domed head peering over. Was she crying? It seemed so by the way a rough sleeve swept at her cheeks.

And then penitence came on him like an illness. Watching Esther cry stripped him of his usual mockery. Here was the remorse which intermittently touched him. Embarrassing when it happened, he railed at it now. The sentimental thing had been roused, making a mouse of him.

A time passed silently.

Black Pat spoke to her in soft adoration. 'One of those happy souls which are the salt of the earth, and without whom this world would smell like what it is – a tomb.'

Esther's voice was puffy. 'Do you mean Michael?'

Black Pat jockeyed himself, needing to take back his professionalism. He seethed at his vulnerability and the chump it made of him.

'I mean me.' He didn't. 'No, I mean you.' Hopeless, he was still clenched with it. So he struggled to clarify, the sorrow in his pulse. 'For what I can regret, I do. And I will regret you, Esther.'

Her sleeve wiped at her cheek and then her chin. 'Who wrote that?'

He nodded gravely. 'I did, I wrote it.' Seeing her complete cynicism he wasted a few seconds, blowing something off his nose, a piece of fluff, his bottom lip extended to aim air at it. He confessed, 'Or perhaps Shelley did.'

Sunday 26 July 1964

33

10.05 a.m.

Clementine had elegant handwriting which looped across the page. She was writing to Randolph at the mahogany desk in the centre of her bedroom, a peaceful figure in a taupe blouse. A photograph of Marigold was positioned on the desk corner. The small white figurine of the maternal goddess Kwan Yin stood on a low shelf above a radiator. From the centre of the mantelpiece, a Louis XVI clock, once belonging to Clementine's mother, kept time with its star-shaped pendulum.

Apart from this ticking and the sound of Clementine's hand moving in fast, irregular bursts over the paper as she wrote, the room was silent.

Next to a box of Italian pencils and a Chinese inkwell on the desk was a glass paperweight in the shape of a pear. A tiny reflection in the pear shifted as something behind Clementine stirred, entering the room. Clementine's eyes had it, steadily holding the reflection, but she didn't move. Her writing slowed fractionally.

There was the cool, smooth sound of a cumbersome leg being put on the salmon-red moiré silk spread of her four-poster bed, then another one. Observing the reflection, Clementine's eyebrows flickered as the intruder jumped its hind legs on the bed and turned round several times, tramping the silk. The intruder's back and humped shoulders brushed the gazebo roof of the four-poster as he moved, then keeling over, covering the mattress. A sloshing started up as the intruder gave the pads of his paws a hot wash, lost in the task, the tongue moving in a rhythmic trance.

'You are distracting me from my writing, I hope you know,' said Clementine.

There was a startled quiet. Then another experimental tongue wipe.

'And I want you to get off my bed immediately,' she said.

The tongue slid back into the mouth with trepidation.

'Off the bed, thank you.'

Black Pat spoke faintly, in shock. 'Can you hear me?'

'I would have thought that was perfectly obvious.'

'You can see me?'

Clementine stopped writing, but didn't turn round. Instead her eyes lifted to regard the dog in the antique gilt gesso mirror hanging above the chimneypiece in front of her. 'This must be quite a surprise for you.'

The silence told her it was a stunning uppercut of a surprise. The dog found her eyes in the mirror. 'Have you always been able to see me?'

'On some level I suppose I have. Will you please remove yourself from my bed? I don't want to have to ask again.'

Black Pat lumped down off the mattress, claws catching the silk and making small scrapes. 'You've never spoken to me before.'

Clementine did turn now, to give the animal the benefit of seeing her determination. 'It's a complicated situation. But this particular visitation of yours is different so I am requesting parley.'

Black Pat's face pulled into a dainty expression of astonishment. 'You want to chat?'

Clementine let out a bristled snort at this. 'No, I do not want to chat. I am calling a temporary truce in order to discuss the terms of this current sabotage on my husband.'

'Right,' Black Pat said meekly. 'Should I come and sit with you?'

'My God, no,' Clementine retorted. 'Stay over there.' She reconsidered. 'Oh, all right, go on then.'

A 1920s dressing table covered in pale pleated silk stood in front of a long window running down the right-hand side of the room. A six-legged stool, painted white, sat in front of the dressing table's mirror. Black Pat pulled the stool to the opposite side of the mahogany desk, then sat. Clementine leant back in her Regency chair, partly to give the dog her full attention, and partly so she could take in his awesome physique at close range. Black Pat looked wild and colossal, his shaggy ruff falling in great sections. He tried to rest an arm on the desk and his elbow hit the box of pencils, the pencils exploding over the floor. Black Pat's hind leg thumped the underside of the desk as he went to collect the pencils. Jumping back, he knocked a copper dish used for holding letters. The dish pitched up and made a dull peal as it hit the carpet.

'Just stop!' Clementine cried as he bent for the dish. 'I'll get it in a minute!' Black Pat cast another squint at the copper dish. A hind paw crept stealthily along the floor towards an escaped pencil, finding it with the toes and attempting to roll it back. The weight of the foot broke the pencil in three, grinding graphite fragments into the cream carpet.

'I almost preferred it when you were on my bed,' said Clementine.

Black Pat said to her sincerely, 'I honestly never realized you knew I was there. In all these years you've never made me even suspect it.'

'Oh, it was quite a challenge, let me tell you,' Clementine told him briskly.

'So what do you want to talk about?'

'I want you to leave this house and let Winston go. I've never asked for anything before, but I am asking you for this, just this once.'

'I can't.'

'You must.'

'It's not in my control.' Black Pat spoke respectfully. Existing in parallel to her for decades had caused him to develop a slight worshipfulness of her talents as an adversary. And despite the fact that Clementine was now elderly, she cowed him.

'Do you know what my husband has to do tomorrow?' Clementine's expression was resolute. 'He has to retire from parliament; he has to retire from his life's work. And don't pretend that you don't know how much this means to him.'

'I know exactly what it means to him,' Black Pat replied.

Folded neatly together, Clementine's hands sat as a dove in her lap. 'Then maybe you could be a friend.'

'I'm not his friend.'

'I don't mean to Winston,' Clementine interrupted. 'Be a friend to me.'

'Oh.' Black Pat's little whiskery brow buds rose.

For a time they watched each other. There was an epic quality in Clementine's stare; it telescoped out and showed the landscape of her emotions. Planted in the centre was the bedrock of her family, not about to go undefended.

'Will you?' she asked. 'Please will you do this?'

'There's nothing I can do for you.'

'Winston is eighty-nine years old. I'm beseeching you to release him, to let him go.'

'You are asking for something I can't give.' Black Pat watched her disappointment, a balloon of remorse swelling in his chest. It made him reflective, circling a possibility and its consequences in his mind. There was no comfort in what he could tell Clementine, but her disappointment made him desperate. Black Pat was unable to look directly at her, her profile a pastel object in his peripheral vision.

'Although,' Clementine heard him say after a while, his voice like midnight in the space between them, 'it would not breach the codes of my contract to notify you that on this occasion my intervention might not be a very prolonged one.'

Clementine brightened, then became suspicious, 'Is this a promise?'

'I don't make promises.' Black Pat urged her not to continue with her questions, the questions leading to heartbreak. He urged her to be satisfied.

'But you will spare Winston?'

There was a pause.

'The only thing I can offer you is the hope that he may not have to endure this for too long.' The span of time allocated to a life was a drop of milk diluting in thin tentacles through the ink of Black Pat, and his answer was duplicitous in a way Clementine could not yet conceive. She would come to in time. 'There is an end to it.' There was an end to everything. 'There is an end to it,' he said again.

She was brittle in her chair. 'Are you telling the truth?'

Black Pat made a compassionate gesture to save her from the truth contained within him. But for Clementine it was enough; it was, for that moment, a victory.

She let out a sigh. 'That's marvellous news.' She started writing again.

Light ran in through the lead-latticed windows and chalked a pattern of diamonds on the floor. Set back in thick stone walls, the windows framed miles of stubbled forest. The room was warmed by the cloudless sky rolling above them. Allowing the tranquillity to overpower him, Black Pat's tail swiped against the stool legs, dragging over the carpet in long brushstrokes.

Hearing the tail, Clementine looked up from the page, the pen still. 'Many thanks for listening to my case.' Her tone was an instruction to leave. Black Pat's tail stopped, hanging dead on the floor.

'. . . You understand this conversation has been a unique occurrence. I won't be talking to you again.'

'I know.'

'And I don't want you to mention this to Winston. It wouldn't be fair if he knew I know about you in the way that I do.' She held her gaze steady. 'It's easier this way, easier on him.'

'You have heard him talk about me . . .'

'Yes, of course. His depression, although private, is no secret. He has often talked about the Black Dog, your visits, your tormenting; it's a very real, very open state.' She swallowed. 'But what you actually are, your hyperreality . . . well, I don't need to tell you it's something he doesn't discuss. So I appeal to you not to say a word to him. This is a confidential conversation, between us only.'

Black Pat accepted it.

Clementine turned back to her writing, a clear statement that the conversation was terminated.

Sliding from the stool, Black Pat started off out of the room. A thought stopped him. He tried to express it sensitively.

'You do realize this won't be the last time you see me, don't you?'

Clementine looked fine and poised, her pussy-bow collar immaculate, the gold earrings handsome next to her cheeks. Around one wrist was a bracelet of pearls. She shook her hand slightly, working the pearls free from her cuff.

'I suspected as much. But even if this isn't the last time I see you, it is certainly the last time I acknowledge you. It'll be exactly as it always has been. It'll appear as though you simply don't exist.'

'Oh,' said Black Pat.

'Quite.'

Clementine had one final point to make. 'You don't intimidate me and you don't intimidate Winston, especially Winston. No, you do not daunt Winston or stunt him. And he has shouldered the burden of your destructive relationship alone and that has been his choice, a brave choice. And it's due to my husband's strength of character that he has been able to withstand it, still achieving what he has.' Clementine stopped to give the dog a precise smile, a smile from the freezer. 'It must be terribly frustrating for you.'

166

'It isn't.' Black Pat was thick with complicated feelings.

She finished, 'I've watched Winston battle against you all these years, and let me tell you, he'll never surrender.'

Black Pat said as he left, 'And you should commend yourself for that.'

34

11.45 a.m.

Corkbowl pressed the car horn and waited outside Esther's house. His tie received a careful straightening, in mathematical alliance with the shirt buttons and ironed with a palm. Esther still hadn't emerged so he gave the horn some cautious taps. Eventually she appeared in whorls through the glass panes of the door, wrestling with the catch.

She was dressed in a green cotton dress and a long-employed camel cardigan, the cuffs flared out into funnels with use. 'Sorry to keep you waiting.'

Around them in the canyons of the seat bases and the foot wells lay the rubble of an old car: sweet wrappers and indistinct dust. In the foundations of the moulded gear stick was a festival of scrunched receipts. The car smelt of fresh herby fish.

Corkbowl explained, starting the ignition and watching for traffic. 'It's a cod dish I made. I offered to bring it to the lunch.' He chatted about cod as they pulled out from the kerb. The car shuddered on its chassis as they waited at a junction, the conversation entirely about cod. Esther nodded along, agreeing, but there was a weird enthusiasm in her answers. Slipping a look at her profile, Corkbowl saw pink scalloped shapes over her cheek and eye. Her lips were the fat animated lips of a person who has been crying.

'Esther, what's wrong?' Unable to stop the car, he sent glances back and forth. Something was wrong.

A wrist scrubbed under her eye. Then a wet laugh full of embarrassment. 'Oh, nothing.'

Corkbowl recognized that she badly wanted him to change the subject. A distraction was needed quickly. The indicator ticked in the dashboard as the car veered right. Corkbowl sifted through the possibilities. Yes, it came to him. He ransacked through the inside pocket of his jacket, one hand sliding about on the wheel. The other hand had retrieved a tiny notepad, a miniature blue plastic pen in the wire spiral binding, the end whitened with chewing. 'I invented something this morning and –' Corkbowl passed over the pad – 'I think it will probably make me a millionaire. Probably definitely.'

She had been saved. Esther felt an elasticated sense of relief. She inspected the drawing. 'Gosh, this is . . .'

The drawing was of a long tube composed of several telescoping pipes, a large flat disc at the top. At the bottom, a curious lump. An arrow informed any interested viewer that the object was fifteen feet in length.

'It's a snorkel.' Corkbowl's finger travelled blindly to the drawing, jabbing around the lump area. 'That's the mouthpiece. It's difficult to draw, which is why it looks a bit . . .' Corkbowl risked a look at the pad, his finger moving to the disc. 'That disc will keep the top of the snorkel afloat. The aerating end will always be above the sea because it floats.'

Esther studied the drawing. The gratitude she felt towards Corkbowl made her very attentive to this madcap snorkel idea. 'Fifteen feet?' A few quick tissue wipes, dabbing away any evidence, back to normal. 'Quite deep, isn't it?'

'*Really* deep. Impressively deep.' Corkbowl tapped at the telescoping pipes. 'But you see, this is the genius of the idea. The snorkel tube extends as you dive, and contracts as you rise up. Forget those short snorkels, bin them, this is a renaissance snorkel.'

'Right,' said Esther. 'The renaissance snorkel.'

'Picture it,' Corkbowl said passionately, 'diving to any level, diving to the seabed with the giant clams!' His hand did a whale dive to illustrate this, dipping to his lap. 'And then diving back up.' This was also illustrated, the whale hand soaring to the car's roof.

Esther smiled at him, a thankful smile which made her look very young.

They pulled into the street, next to Beth and Big Oliver's house. The key came out and the engine died. Corkbowl strained to twist to the rear seat, grappling up the foil-wrapped serving dish balanced there. He sat back with the dish on his legs. 'So . . .' His car door swayed. 'So, shall we?' He hesitated. 'We can sit here for a minute if you want to.' The door drew shut protectively. 'Or . . .'

'No, come on.' She had restored her composure. 'Let's go in.'

Beth bounced to the door as they rang the bell. Her oven gloves welcomed them into the hall, Corkbowl admiring a framed poster of Kenilworth Castle and another hanging near the telephone table of a girl feeding an ostrich. Corkbowl also admired Little Oliver's new toy truck, Little Oliver keen to demonstrate its rotating wheels by driving it up Corkbowl's leg. Wearing his new smart outfit of a gingham shirt and blue trousers, Little Oliver jumped to hug Esther and then stood on his mother's shoes, arms locked around her waist as a waddling Beth ushered Esther and Corkbowl into the kitchen area.

Beth barked for her husband and he appeared with a bottle of white wine.

'Welcome to my humble commode.' As usual here was the joke, as usual Big Oliver loving it.

Big Oliver shook Corkbowl's hand, dealing him the wine bottle which he accepted with a free elbow. Big Oliver subtly herded Corkbowl and his foil cod over to Beth. 'Someone needs to help my wife . . .' he gave a comedian's frown at Beth, a large glass of wine in her oven glove, ' . . . before she helps herself.'

Corkbowl presented his cod and was subjected to voracious praise. For less than a second, only once, was there evidence of collaboration between Beth and Big Oliver. Beth fired a squash ball look at her husband. That was the signal.

'How are you feeling?' Big Oliver squeezed Esther to him, talking mutinously into her ear.

Esther spoke into the wall of his shoulder. 'Not too bad.'

He manoeuvred her by the arms so he could read her expression. 'We're all glad to have you here today.' Another embrace was rough with emotion. 'You're going to get through this, Hammerhans. You will. We'll all get through it.' Beth and Corkbowl were talking. Big Oliver kissed Esther on the cheek. 'The three of us, we'll stick together as we always have.' He was still holding her shoulders. 'Or the two of us.' He shunted his head at Beth. 'Just say the word, we'll ditch her and make a run for it.'

Corkbowl came over with three glasses of wine held in tripod fingers.

'And what's this I hear about you having an audience with Church-ill this afternoon?' asked Big Oliver, opening the conversation to Corkbowl. 'Beth told me and I thought I was hallucinating. Who are you meeting tomorrow? Che Guevara?'

Corkbowl smiled, not so chatty now as there was a stone of embarrassment in his throat. His cod had finished warming in the oven and was ready to be judged. On the other side of the room Beth was busy with a bowl of new potatoes and cauliflower. Down came a dish of peas. She made a cone of her oven gloves and shouted through the cone, 'Come and get it!'

At the table there was the banging of cutlery and friendly bustling as they took their chairs and handed round the food.

Big Oliver talked through a cheek of fish. 'Nice. Good work, Corkbowl.'

'Happy to be of service,' Corkbowl answered, clearly delighted.

Little Oliver didn't want cauliflower, and was forced to have some. 'But I don't like this,' he appealed to his mother.

'Chin up, soldier,' Big Oliver said to him, a massive piece of cauliflower on his fork, 'nobody likes it.'

Corkbowl nodded his agreement and Little Oliver was more or less persuaded. Between mouthfuls he drove his truck around the cruets. When he wasn't looking Beth put a serving of peas in the truck's trailer. Little Oliver was obliged to unload this haul on to his plate and eat his greens.

Beth laughed. 'As the best meal of the week, I think Sunday lunch should always be fun.'

'Absolutely correct,' said Big Oliver.

'It's a serious business, having fun at lunch.' Beth grabbed Esther's and Corkbowl's wrists, solemn doing this, lowering her head in a joking grace. 'Gathered here together, O Lord, let us bray.'

She made a sly survey of their faces. 'Forgive me Father, for I have grinned.'

Even Esther smiled. Big Oliver saw this and lifted his glass, prompting a toast.

'To the chef.'

All glasses met, fragile clinks in a group.

'And . . .' Big Oliver's smile went to Esther, went to everyone, went back to Esther, 'here's to absent friends.'

'Absent friends,' Corkbowl repeated obediently. Beth said the same, sending cautioning eyes to Big Oliver.

'Yes.' Esther put her glass on the table. 'To absent friends.'

The smiles at the table misted. Corkbowl was watching, aware that the awkward colours of the mood converged in streams to the quiet prism of Esther. He sensed a darkness woven into the day, but couldn't divine it. Very slightly Esther's head turned to the garden. Nothing there. She checked again.

Beth rallied herself, needing to rescue Esther. Big Oliver was always a good source of communal amusement. 'Hey,' she said to him and the rest of the group, 'tell Corkbowl about the time you sang on stage with your awful pop group . . .'

Big Oliver knew his instructions. He also knew this story, having polished it over thousands of retellings. 'Corkbowl,' he said, leaning over, 'you appear to be a man acquainted with tragedy, so let me tell you about the tragedy of my university group.'

A laugh of anticipation burst from Beth like popcorn, the story a classic.

'The night had gone badly,' Big Oliver lamented to Corkbowl. 'The songs we'd written . . .' he shook his head, disturbed, ' . . . they had gone badly.' Beth mimed the next line along with him: 'We were staring into the face of desperation.'

'Not a pretty face,' Beth said, as always.

'No,' Big Oliver confirmed, 'not *at all*.'

Beth winked at Esther. And the conversation was stitched together, Corkbowl an audience to the historic group anecdote. Little Oliver had a big announcement; he intended to paint a picture of them all. Esther listened from the edges, glanced at by Corkbowl. They all ate, stray forks moving to claim leftover potatoes from the serving bowl once the plates were empty. Unluckier forks picked at scraps of cauliflower. They fell into the easy nonsense brought on by afternoon wine. But the air bore a smell which distracted Esther. Corkbowl was talking to her and she gave a thin answer. Her laughs were perfunctory and Corkbowl registered it. That smell; Esther hunted around her again, hunting the house from her seat.

Little Oliver was released from the captivity, allowed to leave the table and play for a while. Beth collected the plates. 'Who wants to help me do the washing up?'

'I will,' Esther and Corkbowl said in chorus.

'Anyone?' Beth asked again, lasers on Big Oliver.

173

'I'll help,' repeated Corkbowl.

Beth bent towards Big Oliver. 'No one's going to help me?'

Big Oliver made a grim expression, the expression of someone realizing they are chewing soil. He trailed after Beth to the large kitchen area, quiet and argumentative, questioning her on the purpose of this instant dishwashing. Beth silenced him with a serrated glare, stood at the sink. 'Because I say so.' She poked her chin at Esther and Corkbowl out of earshot in the dining room. 'Because that's the plan.'

Corkbowl remounted his spectacles on to the bridge of his nose with a prod. His finger retracted into its fist on the tablecloth. Next to him Esther was gazing at the garden. The gravitational field of instinct pulled her eyes there.

'Are you okay?' He gave her a friendly bump on the elbow with his own.

She reassured him: yes she was fine.

'Esther, has something happened?' Corkbowl remembered their conversation in the library, remembering the car journey. 'It's just that I don't believe you are okay. Not quite, not really.'

Eyes to the garden. Sketched through with shadows of cedars and poplars, the large garden spread away from the house and merged with the wild border of holly trees that barricaded a tract of public forest. Anchored in the lawn were a bed of flowering bushes and a flat-headed yew, an old kneeling apple tree.

Chatter came faintly from behind them in the kitchen, Big Oliver and Beth piling wet crockery on the draining board.

'I think you might be right, if I'm completely honest.' A smash of cutlery, Big Oliver dropping it into the sink. Then Esther risked a glance at Corkbowl, daring herself. 'Can I tell you about it? I wanted to tell you before, and then . . .' She felt that black mercenary tracking her, a hostile force coming for her fast. 'I don't know if I've got enough time, but . . .' So do it with haste, do it now. 'Corkbowl, do you mind if I tell you?'

'Esther, of course you can.' Corkbowl looked over his shoulder at the kitchen, at Big Oliver taunting his wife, trying to gauge the time they had left alone, not understanding. 'We've got plenty of time.'

But time was up.

A white feather geyser of pampas grass came from the middle of the lawn. And lounging there like a burn in the celluloid was Black Pat.

Very casual, he gave Esther an upward nod. Sitting down, he stood up. He assumed the canine bow of play in a stretch. It was a luxurious stretch, huge in size and sensual. Chest to the floor, his bottom made a black hummock in the sky. Black Pat's face wrinkled with pleasure, flat front legs driving out into the turf. Too relaxing, the process inspired a yawn, the tip of his tongue in an elegant curve. It forced a shrill faint sound: *Yow!*

Fully refreshed, Black Pat sauntered to the French windows. He paused. Moles! His paw raked up a cup of earth.

Esther found her courage and held it steady. She spoke with the soft, determined speed of an impossibly short deadline. 'My husband Michael died two years ago. Today is the anniversary of his death.'

'Oh, Esther.'

'He was a good man, a good husband. He was a brave man.' She smiled and it was just the vapours of a smile. 'He was always very brave.'

Corkbowl heard the raw tone she used. 'Yes.'

'Michael tried so hard, and it matters so much that he did.' Esther stopped. 'Because,' she said, and stopped again.

'Esther?' said Corkbowl.

No, Esther, don't say it. Black Pat willed her not to say the words.

But those words came from her gently. 'He took his own life. Michael committed suicide.'

Esther struggled against Black Pat's ferocious will as she remembered Michael's measured destruction. It had been a long and increasingly desperate fight with a darkness that broke in moonless waves, claiming him for weeks, sometimes more. Esther would wait for her lost husband, a little light on the shoreline waiting to guide him back. And eventually these episodes would fade, retreating in staining tides. Michael would surface, liberated. He was with her. The days would pass. Then: a change. The water would return, thinly at first, a gradual process. Perhaps this time it wasn't going to be so bad. But they could never stop it, and it would start to pour in. Michael wouldn't tell her, he would try and spare her. Neither of them was ever spared. Finally there came the roar of gathering water. A force would draw it into a peaked body, racing on the engine of its own momentum. Michael kept swimming to the little light on the shoreline as the horizon lifted in a great rearing wall.

And Esther's thoughts collected at the end, at how this cycle was ended.

It finished in secluded woodland, nowhere particular, the agony of decision played out in the slow lock of the hammer. The despairing search for release had narrowed and tightened, narrowing finally into the tight dimensions of a steel chamber.

Corkbowl was talking to her, his fingers pressed to his temple. 'Esther, I'm sorry.'

Thank you, Corkbowl: she hurried to thank him.

Black Pat was at the French windows, five panels that folded open on runners. He pressed his snout to the glass and it crooked to make a troll nose, the black nostrils squashed. Finding himself fabulous, he walked into the kitchen, unseen by the others. He accepted Esther's ugly glance as a standing ovation.

'Ha, those two,' Black Pat said, recognizing Beth and Big Oliver over there. 'And *him* again,' he said, recognizing Corkbowl and resentful.

Beth was scraping from a tub of hard-frozen ice cream, serving it into bowls. Big Oliver, a used tea towel slung on his shoulder, got in her way, eating directly from the tub with a stolen wafer.

'Oh, Esther . . .' Corkbowl said, the dog slumped next to her.

Black Pat craned his neck at Corkbowl in a nasty examination. Bound to be hilarious, he smirked at his poem: 'A man such as this is an acquired taste – he'd be decent in chunks, but better as paste.'

'I can't believe it, I'm just so sorry,' Corkbowl repeated.

'It's taken me a long time to understand his depression. I think I do now.' Esther heard the slow applause of a tail. 'I think I've started to.' The applause increased, approving. 'But sometimes I find it –' it was difficult to concentrate through the burr created by the beating tail – 'I find I can't believe it either.' She amended this. 'Well, I believe it here.' Esther touched her forehead. 'But here –' she put a palm on her heart – '*here* it still doesn't make sense.'

'What you just said,' Black Pat choked off a dirty laugh, 'makes sense to me here.' He pointed to his rear end.

Corkbowl said, 'Did Michael ever talk about his depression?'

'Not in any way that let me see the full extent of it. Michael didn't even use the word. He refused to name it.'

'Which offends me . . .' Black Pat moved his paw, deciding, then pointing again at his rear end, ' . . . yes, here.'

Esther recalled to Corkbowl, 'I suppose occasionally I glimpsed how much trouble Michael was in, when he couldn't hide it. It was there in his exhaustion and his face. It was in the atmosphere he had around him. During the worst times the weight of the atmosphere was almost like another presence.'

Black Pat was a giant leering blot in her peripheral vision. You bet it was, thought Esther, the line for him. She said firmly to Corkbowl, 'That's the best way I can think of to describe it, really, as a presence draining him.'

The blot of Black Pat came into focus as he approached Esther, and went out of focus as he got too close. 'I've come to take you home.'

Beth and Big Oliver had rowdily taken their seats at the table, both carrying bowls. 'What are you kids talking about?' asked Beth, the prying aunt.

'Oh, not much,' Esther said, with a faultless performance of sincerity.

'Pudding,' said Corkbowl, taking Esther's cue.

The china bowls held the pale yellow scoops of ice cream, pools of gently melting vanilla. Little Oliver ran back to his chair at full speed, ice cream the king of all foods.

Black Pat put his head on Esther's shoulder, his buffalo weight against her. 'Esther . . .'

'Anyone want more wafers?' said Big Oliver, ramming another into Esther's ice cream. The wafer shattered. ''Scuse fingers,' he grinned at her.

' . . . Is you is –' the damp rubber of Black Pat's nose touched Esther's cheek – 'or is you ain't coming home?'

Corkbowl realized the time. 'Esther, umm . . . I hate to mention it. We'll need to leave soon if we're going to get to Churchill's on time.'

'Ah!' said Big Oliver. 'But the hour cometh, and now is.'

Esther and Churchill. Black Pat looked sharply at Corkbowl. He gave the same cheated look to Esther. The prospect of her meeting Churchill was a ticklish one. His breath made a hot bloom on her skin, urgent now. *Listen to me, listen to me.*

The heat of his head was sordid, the stink of him in her nose and mouth, that sea cucumber of a tongue channelling its rot-scented whispers into her ear. Beaten, Esther said to Corkbowl, 'I'm not sure I can go to Kent.'

'*Yes.*' Beth misinterpreted the statement. Her warm hand was affectionate, gentle squeezes convincing Esther's arm. 'We can sort it out. You stay here with us if you'd rather.'

'You should go home.' This boiled down her ear.

'Perhaps I should go home.'

'With me, Esther.'

'You want to be on your own today?' It worried Big Oliver. 'Wait, you want to be on your own?'

Beth went to follow as Esther left the room and was restrained by Big Oliver. They bickered animatedly between themselves, a hushed argument over what to do. It was interrupted by a bang of knees on the table legs, Corkbowl on his feet. Two blank faces stared at him.

'Let me go after her,' he said softly.

Their stares pursued him into the hall.

Esther was pulling on her baggy cardigan.

'Hi.' A step took Corkbowl closer. 'Do you want to talk more about it?'

Black Pat had cornered her by the front door. Corkbowl agitated him, making his hackles spike. Esther's reply was pathetic. 'Thanks for asking, but I don't want to bore you. I'd better be off.'

Corkbowl ran a wrist over his mouth, checking for ice cream. No, it was found to be clean so he asked if she was sure.

'I don't know.' She slung her bag on a shoulder and it fell. 'I wish I knew.'

'I'll tell you what I know. I do know this.' Corkbowl braved another step. Go on, he thought, go on, say your stupid embarrassing quote. He rushed it out: 'Those friends thou hast . . . grapple them unto thy soul with hoops of steel.'

This Corkbowl . . . Black Pat was sickened. He threw a look of ridicule at Esther and noted no similar sneer.

'Right,' Esther said to Corkbowl, politely confused.

Corkbowl blushed over an explanation. 'It's basically an incoherent way of saying that I'm your friend . . .' A bit presumptive, he corrected it. 'I hope we can become friends . . . umm.' He said honestly, 'I'm ready to do anything I can to help.' Corkbowl slapped his thigh – a sign the next statement would mortify them both. 'I suppose, in essence, I'm trying to steel-hoop you.'

179

It didn't just mortify Esther and Corkbowl. It also marked a shift in Black Pat, rousing a possessiveness in him. Esther, he realized, would be a more strenuous win than he had assumed. Fine, the result would be the same. But there was rivalry in Black Pat's voice as he asked Esther, 'You like Shakespeare? Here's a bit of Shakespeare: a man may fish with the worm that hath eat of a king, and eat of the fish that hath fed of that worm.'

Corkbowl's steel-hoop comment had found a curiously receptive audience in Esther. Black Pat's worm comment was a mystery.

'It's basically an incoherent way,' Black Pat said, imitating Corkbowl in a lunatic pitch, 'of saying that . . .' he curled his face, 'I'll not be exorcized so easily. Now *that* you know.'

An inaudible countdown was going on in the kitchen, counting down to Beth and Big Oliver coming to investigate. The group in the hall understood this. Black Pat reminded Esther of her orders to return home with a shin-kick of his muzzle and was rewarded with complete rebellion.

'I don't want to go home,' she told them in a sudden blurt. 'I don't want to go there.'

'Where do you –'

Esther's solution was immediate: 'Well, I guess we did agree to go to Kent . . .'

Corkbowl's face registered his surprise. 'Yes, of course, Kent.'

The car keys were in his pocket, warm from his leg. He rummaged to release them.

'You won't come home?' A spark of acute rejection. Black Pat's muzzle flickered in a grimace. 'Not that it matters either way.'

Esther opened the door, she was leaving. The dog trailed behind as they went to the car. 'Because I'll be wherever you are, Esther.'

'See you later, alligator,' Black Pat called after her, his showmanship slightly compromised. He watched Corkbowl's car, nearly glum as it disappeared. 'See you in a tick, tick,' he called experimentally to no one.

35

In his bedroom, a small, plain room annexed from the study, Churchill was asleep in bed, hands drawn across his waist, cradling his round tortoiseshell spectacles in a loose handshake.

Black Pat went over, putting out his head, sniffing tamely. The smell of cigars mingled with the palette of a large elaborate lunch. Port and French cheeses had been involved. What else? He leant closer, decoding the scents of consommé, Dover sole, champagne and the deluxe personality of chocolate éclairs.

Suddenly Churchill was awake, glasses hooked over his ears in an instant. He shouted out to find the dog hanging over him and then pulled himself into a sitting position, heaving up the pillows.

Black Pat lay down on his side, a black mass covering the floor. The weight of the giant body pressed on the lungs, driving out a foul cloud. The dog's head slipped round to the bed, vanishing beneath it.

Churchill poured himself a glass of whisky from a decanter on the bedside table, thinning it with soda water. He took a mouthful and his teeth bit together at the taste, whisky moving in a smooth stream to his stomach. Churchill sipped for a while and analysed a docile rasping noise. He realized it was the dog gnawing on a bed leg, its carnassial teeth sawing against the oak.

'Stop that!'

The dog's lazy head appeared.

Churchill arranged himself in a more comfortable position, dragging the edges of his exotic red and gold Chinese silk dressing gown around him. Thinking again of tomorrow, he let the crab claws of his imagination make exploratory nips over Monday's agenda, investigating the shape of it. And it was as if the events of the day were already in the past, so perfectly could he envisage it: the view through the window during the car journey; the passing landmarks solemn with poignancy; Big Ben rising through the nearing skyline; the sound of shoes on gravel as they walked to the entrance. He heard the journalists' retrospective questioning echoing across the bellying crevices of his mind, and talked roughly to his watery whisky.

'Stitch yourself together.'

'I see your thoughts.' Black Pat propped a shoulder against the bed, his head making a grave of the bed sheets as it sank in. 'The eyes are a window to the soul and I see them all.'

'Hah, obnoxious clown,' Churchill said, turning to look at him, a defiant smile twitching. 'In that case your eyes are a derelict staircase leading to a barren landing.' He drank from the glass, lip pushed whitely to the rim. Draining the whisky, the glass went down with a firm clunk on the side.

'I remind myself continually not to perform autopsies on the future, but I admit I cannot prevent myself. It is an irremediable flaw.'

'You should treat yourself kindly,' Black Pat said from the sheets. 'You should let yourself listen to the compulsions that drive you to do it.'

'Gammon!' Churchill reached behind his head to tug a pillow higher against the headboard. 'I can't bear the sound of my own voice, it won't quiet. And it talks with such gloom, wanting to pauperize me. No, I won't listen. As Oscar Wilde said, don't squander the gold of your days listening to the tedious.'

He said this with an underlying sense of futility, looking at a vase of oxeye daisies Clementine had placed on his windowsill, put there with love and springing with life. He thought of Clementine's hands picking them, dear hands among the leaves.

'Do you know what my wife says to me during these periods when you are around? She calls me a poor old thing.' A ripple of air caught the petals and they fluttered their tips with the draught. 'Although sometimes I wonder which of us is really the poor old thing . . .' Churchill frowned. 'It's an enduring bruise on my conscience that our vile alliance has had such impact upon her. I worry about the sacrifices she has made for me, aware that I can't hope to repay them, and the gratitude terrifies me. It devours me.'

The empty glass smoked with fumes, the scent of whisky drawing Black Pat to the bedside table, sidling there. His craving snout came within inches then ducked inside, wet against the deep glass base.

Churchill noticed. 'That is Johnnie Walker Red Label, an exemplary blended Scotch. And not a drink I would offer to you.' He added, 'I'd rather use it to kill my plants.'

Black Pat made a smooch of his mouth, amused. The glass was released, banged across the tabletop and then left perilously on the edge. That hog from the quag! Churchill nudged the glass to safety with a finger.

Footsteps outside the door paused, a knuckle rapping before the handle bent and his nurse and factotum Roy Howells entered with a pot of fresh coffee.

Howells moved busily, the carpet an invisible network of circuits he had travelled every day for years: to the bedside table; to the wardrobe; to the bathroom; to the window.

'It's nearly time for your afternoon bath, sir. Should I set the taps running?'

'Very good, Howes,' said Churchill, using the customary nickname. 'Thank you.'

Howells disappeared into the adjoining bathroom, the taps blasting into the tub.

Jock had strolled in behind Howells. With a graceful bounce the cat landed on the bed, rubbing its head on Churchill's arm. Catching sight of Black Pat, it jacked up its back and spat.

'Quite right, Jock,' Churchill smiled. 'My sentiments exactly.'

The cat was vicious, a small orange warrior. Caught by surprise Black Pat whickered, his heavy head dodging the threshing claws.

'Keep buggering on,' Churchill said encouragingly.

'Me?'

'Not you, you poltroon, I was talking to Jock. I would much rather you keep buggering *off*.' Churchill let out a sigh, adding, 'But I know how empty that statement is.'

Black Pat's expression was entertained and then broke, a deeper feeling in him lit across his face in a ghost. 'I will be accompanying you tomorrow.'

'Yes.' The cat wound under Churchill's hand and then twisted back. 'It would trouble me if you didn't.'

36

4.50 p.m.

On either side of Chartwell's front door was an elaborate eighteenth-century doorcase, carved wooden pillars decorated with overlapping leaves, two carved horns sending up a spray of wooden vines. It was a subtle introduction to the artistic investment made in the house by the owners. There on the doorstep were Corkbowl and Esther.

'You can do it, champ.' Corkbowl gave her a gentle smile.

She nodded at him, an anxious champ.

Howells invited them in and they stood in the narrow hall, quietly examining the giant visitors' book placed on the walnut dresser. The book was guarded by a bronze of a thoroughbred horse. A mahogany umbrella stand held a collection of walking sticks.

Esther received instructions from Howells: he would take her to Churchill's study presently. She was not to stay too long, as Churchill would need rest later. Corkbowl had his own instructions; he would be quarantined in Clementine's study until required to drive Esther home. Both would receive tea if they wanted. Did they want tea? Then this would be arranged.

Up the stairs went Howells, Esther following. The staircase was a series of sharp corners, framed political cartoons over the walls and photographs, Lord Kitchener in one of them, which seemed appropriate. On the landing Howells cruised in front, his steps snatching lengths of precious carpet as he led Esther to the study. Esther tried to dawdle, to drag back some seconds. It was hopeless, Howells too efficient, already knocking on the study door. An inquisitive noise bid them entry, Churchill in his chair. He was the man she knew from the newspapers and television, older than she had imagined him although she knew his age. That famous voice was still mostly unchanged and it would address her personally. Being star-struck was a flighty feeling, Esther a bit giddy with it.

'Esther Hammerhans, sir.' Howells heeled neatly and was gone.

Esther held her bag in a white fist.

'Ah, excellent.' Churchill indicated a small table set up near his desk. On it was a typewriter, made to be silent, and a ream of stacked paper. A straight-backed chair was ready for her.

Esther crept to the table. About to ask a question to ease the silence, she remembered Dennis-John's instructions and didn't. Instead she prepared the typewriter, a long procedure.

The arm of Churchill's spectacles was in his mouth. Out it came. 'You have completed your preparations?' He was keen to start. This was a difficult afternoon, pleasureless. He tasted the apprehension like chemical smoke in his throat, knowing they would probably be joined by that maddening numbfish. It was more than probable. 'Should we begin?'

She was ready, yes, smiling and pleasant. But something about Esther disturbed him. Hello, what's this? There was a quality to her, a recognizable . . . Hmmm. His radar identified the property and monitored it. Yes, a strange energy about her, a dying star in the sky of her face.

Unaware, Esther sat at her small table. She privately toured the room from her chair. Above the door to the stairs hung a painting by John Lewis Brown, titled *Two Cavalry Officers*. One officer in a cream jacket raised a strict arm at the officer in red, the red officer with his back to the viewer. Studying the painting Esther emoted with the faceless red officer, seeing him there on his slovenly horse. A quick glance at Churchill saw he was looking at the gardens, looking away from her. Reassured, she started the tour of his study again.

Churchill was evaluating his thoughts. Unusual thoughts, Churchill dismissed them. 'Pox-rot,' he chastised himself. 'Bunkum.'

His mental focus returned to the speech, this abomination of a chore. The speech had to be aggressively approached; a task to throw over by the ankle. Bah, start the thing, he lectured his reluctant mood, and shuffled papers on his desk.

For a few silent moments Churchill thumbed through the card catalogue of his past, resolving an introduction. Esther poised at the typewriter and then he had it, the words found. A sentence was dictated.

Useless with nerves she typed out a string of nonsense. 'Oh I'm so sorry, I've . . .' Perhaps if she used the correction fluid. She reached for it and was stopped.

'No matter.' Churchill gave her a game nod. 'We shall relaunch. Take that sheet and confound it to the floor.'

The act of throwing the crushed paper, littering Churchill's carpet: Esther smiled at how much Dennis-John would purple. She visualized this purple Dennis-John as the paper became a ball. Over it went, now there on the floor. More paper was fed into the platen knobs, the paper bail reset. The mood between Churchill and Esther warmed from the difficult distance of strangers. They became two unenthusiastic and melancholy allies driven together to complete a duty. Churchill took in a breath, drove it out, took in another, started again. The psalm melody of his words tolled over the beams. It was a speech of compassion for his country, a farewell to his career.

Esther hunched to type, the alphabet printing through the ribbon. They fell into a rhythm of concentration. And then it happened.

Footsteps. Deviant steps. Esther gambled a look at the study door. In soaked the distinguished stink. Her eyes dealt an ill stare at Churchill. What should they do? Esther watched Churchill for clues. His frown had formed dour hooks. The intensity of Esther's watching caught his attention and he repaired the gap in his dictation, moderating his frown, believing she was waiting for him to continue.

'Let us not be men of straw.' A grey smile from Churchill. 'We should keep going if we are to finish this damned exercise.' And they carried on.

Awful, the door eased open. In he walked, that beast. He walked with a pantomime sneak, careful not to wake the children, this Santa Claus from the underworld. Black Pat was using a quavering voice, the voice of a very elderly woman, singing 'Tiptoe Through the Tulips'.

Esther tried to focus as Churchill spoke. It was useless. Black Pat performed his way across the room and bashed down like a sack in between them. A grin fought the seal of his lips.

Churchill noticed the direction of Esther's gaze. No. No, she couldn't see it. Behave, he told himself. Behave logically, by Jehovah.

Esther acted normally and was a terrible actor. The smiling secretary, she gave Churchill a smile and searched through the options. All options were poor: Churchill could see Black Pat – it was certain, Esther knowing this absolutely. But what of her ability to do the same? Esther wanted to shout it out and be bankrupt. She wanted to clench Churchill's hand and tell him she knew, to grip his cuff in a hard twist and tell him.

Instead she did nothing. The noble action was no action, for to discuss the dog would violate a guarded privacy, exhuming the bones of a family of secrets. It would be grave robbery. The dog's genius was to make orphans of hope and brotherhood, and she was united with Churchill in their isolation.

Esther feigned consummate ignorance. She swiped with the small clogged brush of correction fluid, making a job of it. She told herself briskly that no black dog was in the room, no black animal had discovered the ball of crushed paper and was toying with it, no giant nose sporting with a soggy paper ball.

Lying on his side Black Pat sent the ball tumbling. He bunted his body after it, claws driven into the carpet as he dragged on his stomach. Claiming the paper, his prize was to eat it. Noisy and disgusting, his happy jaws mashed the ball into a fibrous slop. Esther instructed herself to be completely unaware.

Churchill slowly worked the hinge of a spectacle arm, wondering. He was supremely talented at concealing his acknowledgement of the dog, suffering with the self-discipline of a samurai. But this Esther Hammerhans was less experienced. The kicking glances she sent, those unintentional jumps of her hands, they were a log of revelations. Here was another one – Esther's cemetery expression as that louche bastard tongued her shoe, drawn there by a fascinating scent. Another revelation came in her tight blast of annoyance as the beast knocked her with his huge head.

Impossible. But could it be possible? No, it was unquantifiable. Churchill reached a conclusion and tore it up. He came back to the same conclusion and sat with it. Might it be that she could see this living expletive, this gimcrack kraken, this . . . Churchill restrained his wrath, putting a stilling hand on it. Keep studying, be sure. A discreet slap as Esther threw Black Pat's reeking paw from her shoulder, and she was found out.

Esther bobbed from the paw, begging between locked teeth, 'Stop it.'

Black Pat said, 'Don't think I will,' the clowning paw going for her shoulder.

Churchill put a thumb to his lip. Esther was new to the four-legged poison, that much was obvious. It was clear in her anxiety, the shock of it still fresh. A few days at an estimate, a week, certainly the first time. Yet the dog was upon her. And he had done much already, his passion betrayed in those loving little looks. Churchill saw it as he had seen it in others. His father, his daughters, his son. Himself. And if given time the animal would thin her down in the same way, for what the dog captured it possessed and starved. So then what? A matter this sensitive required rare tactics. Toe forwards, Churchill thought. Toe forth. He said with extreme care, 'Some days, such as

189

this one, I find about as beguiling as a breakfast of death cap toadstools.'

He observed her. Was she with him? It seemed not, her cheeks stewing with embarrassment as she ignored Black Pat. Difficult to ignore, the dog dived around on the floor, chasing her shoelaces and grunting.

'For some days seem to offer only the promise of spreading increasing discomfort to the days ahead.' Churchill made a purse of his mouth. 'I thought I'd mention it; my suspicions told me you may understand what I mean.'

No, not quite. Esther waited for more. Black Pat also waited, the shoelaces forgotten.

'It's during these unforgiving times,' said Churchill, 'I can discover I'm permitting myself to lurch into a state of *nostalgie de la boue*.'

'Sorry, de-la-what? Nosta-what?'

'It literally translates,' Churchill told her, 'as a longing for mud, a curious appetite for depravity. For me it's caused by the occasions when I turn to the horizon and see advancing an army of storms. In the presence of overwhelming apprehension thoughts can tempt towards surrender, towards accepting direct defeat.'

Esther's finger bent and met a key on the typewriter, tapping there. If she understood correctly then this was a veiled reference to Black Pat. Here was an unusual dilemma.

'But,' above the tortoiseshell spectacles Churchill studied Esther, 'this *black* mental annotation is not to be viewed as truthful, it is only a kink in the link.' He stopped to gauge how far to push it. They were on tender ground. He urged her to meet his taciturn advances with her own.

Black Pat wasn't playing any more. He lay on the floor, quiet and dangerous.

She spoke at last. 'I've heard that phrase before.'

'I'll wager that you have.' Churchill let her watch him clip a clear, patent glance at the dog. 'And it's not all you'll have heard.'

So they were talking about their mutual companion. Esther absorbed this. In it went, this uniquely weird information. Then out it came, too weird to be retained. Black Pat's sense of caution was tuned on all frequencies, a powerful attitude radiating from him.

Churchill added, 'And to anyone who has listened to such falsehoods, I would advise this: mendacity is bilge, mendacity through a bullhorn is merely loud bilge.'

'Loud bilge . . .' Esther sounded apologetic.

'I fancy I'm trying to express that what seizes our attention is not always what should hold our attention.' Very steadily Churchill's gaze brewed. 'For, Esther Hammerhans, the demands made on us by corruptive forces can sometimes be challenging to filter. We can believe we are making a choice based on the evidence placed before us, but it's not a choice if the evidence comes from a goon community.'

Churchill paused, distracted by the surprising difficulty of the subject. Ah, a new angle.

'It should be stated that the blackest words deserve no more heed than intestinal wind.'

Should it be stated? Esther worked at this statement in a heroic effort not to laugh, moderately successful.

He said, 'Do you follow?'

'I nearly follow. Maybe if . . .' The words tactfully died out.

'Har.' Churchill relayed his arguments back to himself, finding them comically obscure. A valiant attempt, yes, but at an abstract tilt. He gave it another shot.

'In every life's landscape there are prairies and caverns . . .' a hesitation dithered and then drove on, ' . . . and a path cuts into the recesses as well as the highland. Some paths cut far further than others, cutting into deep caves.' Churchill registered his name whispered from the floor. He snubbed it. 'And so be it, if that's the course. But I would never venture to the caves if other options were available to me, and should this be the solitary option I would still exhaust all spirit resisting.' A scowl aimed quickly at the whispering, threatening it. 'And more than that, above all else, I dearly hope I would perform no action which assisted these darker journeys. If it happens then I strive to tolerate it, however, I will never consent to the descent.'

'Which can get tiresome.' Dry and flat, Black Pat's voice came from the floor and got no attention.

Esther listened to Churchill.

'Stand firm. Offer no help, no hand to . . .' Churchill broke off, setting his jaw in determination, ' . . . to the hostile forces who would have you do otherwise.'

The dog moved one of his hind legs and made a flabby sound. Esther wasn't interested in him. Inside her a tiny but voracious optimism sent out its horns. She looked at Churchill and looked away. She looked at Black Pat and speculated. She looked at the past few days and saw the coming days differently. Black Pat goofed about, keen to divert her. Hard to divert, he leant his head and took a clump of Esther's skirt. Delicious, he gave it a tug. The skirt pulled taut to the point of ripping.

Churchill mourned that she didn't have the spice to thrash the dog. Thrash him, he silently commanded, as Esther wrestled her skirt with dainty fury. That retaliation, thought Churchill, has the spice of white bread.

'May I proffer some immediate advice?' he said to her, watching from his chair. 'Take immediate action.'

How to do this . . . a complex task when in company, the rules of the situation prohibiting an overt action. Esther took an indecisive swig from her cup of tea. The skirt fell from Black Pat's teeth as he became suspicious, the speed at which she drank needing inspection. He leaped up to crane at the cup. Perhaps, thought Black Pat, the tea is laced. An explanation, a good one. His nostrils sent a report from the rim of the mug and declared him a romantic fool. Black Pat went sullenly back to the floor.

Although it was an action of sorts, it was totally, bonelessly spiceless. Churchill popped his knuckles, widely unconvinced it would endure. Before him on the desk was a photograph of Clementine taken when she launched the aircraft-carrier HMS *Indomitable*. The monochrome photograph showed her from the waist, face turned high, a white smile, the brimless hat worn at an angle. Here she was, his Clementine, the beautiful shadow of her jawline leading to an elegant earring as she smiled at the HMS *Indomitable* twenty-four years ago. It was aptly a favourite photograph, a crucible image which seared off all but the sense of rushing, rooted love and the word *indomitable*. An exceptional pairing, Churchill thought, steeling in times when the stomach was unhorsed.

Remembering Clementine, Churchill also remembered the speech. That cursed thing still needed to be hacked out. And Clementine, she would want him down for dinner. 'Clementine,' he said, 'will be expecting an opus, the time we've spent here. How much have we got?'

Left to form her own trance, Esther snapped out of it. 'About a paragraph. But if I scratch off the correction fluid we could stretch it to a page.'

'That's a plan B,' answered Churchill. 'B for bumptiously bad.'

'Right,' said Esther. 'Let's start again.'

Yes, Churchill agreed, it called for a new sheet. 'Otherwise your team at home will be gathering reinforcements, about to begin a search.'

'Sadly not.' Esther gave him the breezy non-smile. 'There's not much of a team since I now live there alone.' Here came an admission: 'Practically alone.' Here came another one: 'There used to be two of us with my husband Michael.' The final admission was a clue, her eyes underlining it. 'Although Michael would have perhaps argued that there were three.'

Churchill translated the hieroglyphics of this statement. The tone she used was a rich description and the picture expanded swiftly. 'Presumably he had a guest?'

Esther said yes and then changed it. 'In the way that guests stay in a home which is not theirs. In that way, yes. Not in the typical way of necessarily being invited.'

'That's the thorny issue with unbidden guests,' said Churchill. 'They can be sweetness itself, refreshing company and a radiant surprise, or they can prove to be . . . ' he allowed himself a ginger grin, ' . . . a *bête noire.*'

Black Pat preened at this, basking. '*C'est vrai.*'

Esther was folding a piece of paper, creating an origami nothing. 'But what –' she said and lost her thread. He hesitated for her to find it. Instead she said, pleasing Black Pat, 'Should we continue with the dictation?' Too hard to talk of, her nerve had failed. 'Otherwise,' she tried to make light of it, 'we'll be typing and dictating all night.'

'Shepherd's delight,' said Black Pat.

Fair enough, Churchill agreed. And the valedictions commenced.

Black Pat schemed from his carpet position. This transference of notes between Churchill and Esther, this delicately coded support . . . he sensed a delinquency in her, in both of them.

'I wanted to let you know . . .' Esther's typing slowed and ended. She spoke quietly to Churchill, 'that it's been very provoking to meet with you today, despite whatever else today has been.'

'Yes,' said Churchill. 'Good.'

The speech took up again and stalled as he registered what she'd said. 'Provoking?' Then understanding it he didn't wait for an answer. 'Yes, provoking. Good.'

He was encouraged. She was provoked; it was a positive in a void of negatives. Churchill's mind went again to the others who had been exposed to these negatives, to those dearest people in his family. And his heart projected images of darling Diana, his oldest daughter, driven to the night's depth last October. The cruelty of this malediction and its fanged hangman was enough to tear holes in the psyche. But there were poultices to fill these holes, tricks to stay afloat. Churchill, his eyes on the HMS *Indomitable*, would jab at the provocation in Esther. He would stoke it. Yes, he thought, keep drilling. A duty, he would uphold it.

'Well, you know what they say,' Churchill said. 'You know what they say if life hands you lemons.'

'Snack on the hand?' volunteered Black Pat.

'Lemonade,' said Esther, confident. 'Make lemonade.'

'They say,' Churchill finished, 'at least you are armed with tough-skinned lemons. Yes, strong yellow projectiles.'

Esther hid a laugh.

'And,' said Churchill, 'if life hands you flies . . .' a nod came to verify it, reasonably amused, 'make *stock*. And then fling it at your enemies.'

A remarkable attitude, but surely not feasible. Esther recalled the boxroom conversation with Black Pat, their twinned orbits, his blameless reaction to a reaction which originated from her. She said, 'I don't know if I have an enemy especially, because I feel –' she put an emphasis on this word, emphasizing that it wasn't her feeling but an instruction – 'I *feel* that I'm the instigator, if you like, of any . . .' How to say this? ' . . . of any handed lemons, and so I've got to accept it.'

'Never.' Churchill's words were fast and stern. 'You must hurl yourself into opposition, for you are at war.'

'No, Esther.' Black Pat pawed her shin.

She moved the shin tightly behind her chair. 'A war?'

'Not a war, Esther,' Black Pat murmured at her.

Churchill said, 'On that you must trust me. From your withering depths to your wuthering heights, you are at war.'

'We are fighting on the same side,' Black Pat said in a pledge. 'Fighting together.'

'And,' said Churchill, hearing, 'you must trust me that you are fighting alone. Esther Hammerhans,' his urgency was a prayer, 'do not consent to the descent.'

For a moment Black Pat was silent. Then he recovered, speaking to Esther and malignant.

'Very stirring,' he said softly. 'It reminds me of a joke I just invented on the spot about this exact situation . . .' He smirked at her and it was ugly. 'There are two men on a sinking ship and one man says to the other, "Do you know how to swim?" The second man replies that he doesn't, so the first man says, "Neither do I, but I'll hold your head up if you hold mine."'

'Disregard it,' said Churchill. 'Disregard all the propaganda, it's a quicksand strategy.'

'Except that it's the truth.' Black Pat's snout went to an area near her foot, and then on it. 'Ahoy,' he said from the pillow of her shoe. 'Ahoy.'

A knock on the door. Howells, keen for Churchill not to tire himself, tactfully enquired about whether Churchill would require a place to be laid at the table.

Howells had a list of questions about dinner. Friends were visiting and would be here shortly. Esther sensed Howells' frogmarching eyes on her and obediently started packing to leave. The speech was passable, it would suffice. Churchill folded it into quarters to be stowed in his breast pocket, Howells returning back downstairs. Esther walked to the door. There she went, now stopping to make a courteous comment about a Swiss clock placed in the bookcase at the door. Esther admired its delicate machinery, impossibly miniature mechanisms swinging highlights on their brass edges.

'A gift from the people of Switzerland. It's a perpetual movement design by Jaeger-LeCoultre.' Churchill's expression was wistful. 'It's a funny thing, the objects that resonate in your life. Not always the ones you expect, and not always in the way you expect.'

Esther saw he was circling a strip of metal in his hands, an item picked from the windowsill museum next to his desk. A thumb swept over the engraving, polishing it.

'It's a piece of shrapnel,' Churchill explained. 'Part of a twenty-pound shell from the First World War.' The fond thumb rubbed. 'Would you believe this dropped between my cousin the ninth Duke of Marlborough and me.' He paused at the memory, amazed. 'We could have been extinguished, easily scrubbed from existence.' A sage smile aimed at Esther. 'But we were able to decline that particular invitation to take a seat in the kingdom. And later my cousin gave me this shrapnel, inscribed, ahhm –' here Churchill adjusted his spectacles, peering at the faint silver letters – 'ah yes . . . "This fragment fell between us and might have separated us for ever, but is now a token of our union."'

The shrapnel was placed on the desk. 'That is as it may be. However, on occasion I consider the phrase apt for other reasons.'

A goring, hate-filled glare surprised Black Pat, still sprawled across the floor.

'For it occurs to me,' said Churchill, 'that this phrase applies to the cohesion I seek in myself.' A second glare was held and then dissolved. 'It can appear to me that my life is splintered into disparate sections, Mayday afternoons and gloaming banishment. Such a cycle cannot be broken, and the battle is not with fighting to accept, but with accepting to fight. It is in doing this, to use a phrase I have used before, that we still are captains of our souls.'

He said to Esther as she stood in the doorway, his final mission statement, 'My endurance of the buckle-end welts which existence has dealt me is a token of union with myself. You see, I unite my past and present, and I therefore survive intact.'

Esther nodded, uncertain, then nodding and sure. 'I do see.'

Churchill smiled at her, seeing her steel. 'Magnificent, ah, Hammer-hans. Let us be beaten and jump up nonetheless, giving the Bronx cheer.'

37

6.35 p.m.

Churchill selected a cigar and pierced the end with a match. He didn't give much notice to the voice speaking from the floor.

'Leaving her isn't something I can do.'

Churchill put the cigar between his teeth and lit it. There was the tiny sound of tobacco flakes catching and smouldering in orange crumbs. He took some enquiring puffs and exhaled. The smoke made a jet through the air. He said to Black Pat, watching as the smoke melted, 'There is a chance she could leave you, though.'

'Not now.' Black Pat heard a car starting up in the driveway at the front of the house. He went to the window, looking down at Cork-bowl's Morris Minor reversing and then arching to the lane. 'Despite your Sermon on the Mount she's –'

Churchill interrupted. 'Not the Mount, it was a sermon from the front. You make us soldiers-in-arms, she and I.'

Black Pat answered from his window, 'She doesn't know that.'

'You underestimate her.' Churchill admired the embers. 'And it's to her credit that she underestimates you.'

38

6.45 p.m.

'Well?' Corkbowl ducked in his seat to see Chartwell House disappearing behind a curtain of forest, the road in a curve. 'How was it?'

The evening lit everything in cinema colours, the car in a ravine below the risen banks of tall beech and oak trees. Red dried earth showed in patches through the trunks, ivy draped in sheets over fallen logs. Corkbowl had opened the windows, letting the heat escape from the baked car.

Esther wafted her neck, wafting her forehead, a futile breeze from the wafting. 'It was okay, yes. It was . . .' She spoke profoundly to her handbag, talking to it as she wedged it in the foot well, 'enlightening.'

'Excellent,' said Corkbowl.

A beat of silence. Both voices came at the same moment. Corkbowl insisted she go first.

'I just wanted to thank you,' she smiled, 'for driving me here today.'

Corkbowl did one of his speciality sidelong glances, a hairy little look. 'It's been my pleasure.'

'Devoting your Sunday to chaperoning me around? You're easily pleased. I don't think many people would be crazy about the idea.'

'Then I'm crazily pleased,' said Corkbowl. He tried out an alternative. 'I'm easily crazed.' This didn't work. 'I think I'll stick with the mortifying steel-hoop statement from Beth's hallway.'

Esther remembered it. She stared out of the window, ferns sending bright young growth from nests of desiccated fronds.

'It's a lovely thing to hear, if a little unusual considering that I'm not exactly at my most . . .' She was unsure how to explain it. 'I don't have much of a capacity for . . .' It trailed into nothing again.

Corkbowl stepped in. 'All friends are a luxury.'

'I'm afraid my friendship is a bit of a strange luxury.'

'So are oysters,' Corkbowl said immediately.

Shades of dark green and red, the ivy covered in red dust at the edges of the road, this area unchanged for centuries. Rounding a corner the small road straightened, a view of more trees ahead before another corner, shadows between the branches revealing slim channels into the woods. And there, a dark shape.

'I doubt it would be classified in the same league as an oyster,' Esther said. 'If we're using those terms then I would probably have to admit to being a bad substitute.'

'Like a vegetable oyster,' Corkbowl answered, with a bizarre answer for everything.

The landscape opened up into a stretch of fields, closing again as the car met a wooded hill, moving up over the coiling roads. Esther watched the trunks block and then break with short patches of the red earth, seeing further into the woods, into the evergreen caves, decaying trees lined with drifts of brown leaves. And up ahead, something.

'It's another name for salsify.' Corkbowl laughed at his own oddness. 'In case you're wondering, I've got a million more bits of rubbish trivia, and I'm not afraid to use them to illustrate all my arguments.' Holding the steering wheel, he shrugged with an elbow. 'Anything you say, I can mash on a confusing, irrelevant analogy.'

A quick glance at Corkbowl, a friendly taunt: 'I had noticed that, yes.'

The figure at the edge of the wood ahead, plashing his jaws, the tongue stroking against the roof of the mouth and hanging in a pant; he waited for the car.

'Yep, thought you might,' said Corkbowl. 'I've got the social dexterity of this.' He put his fist out and held it rigidly. Not rigid enough, he said, 'No, of that,' and pointed to a stone wall.

Short laughter. 'Oh, you're not that bad . . . I'd have placed you on a much higher social level.' Esther made a swimming fish with one hand to demonstrate the flexible level.

The car came past, driving in an easy crawl as Corkbowl chatted. Black Pat moved with a pack-animal gait, moving alongside the car, now veering to probe a fallen branch, now back at the car. Esther kept her eyes away from him. Inspired to lick the half-open passenger window, the gruesome textures of Black Pat's tongue swerved over the glass.

Corkbowl had seen Esther's swimming hand. 'Not even close, I'm afraid.' The next sentence had a secret woven into it: 'Nope, if you came with me for a drink I could prove it to you.'

Esther's head turned to him. She saw his profile very concentrated on driving.

The car slowed to a plod, navigating a shallow pit in the road. Black Pat had slipped behind, walking parallel with the rear of the car and dawdling. Esther checked him in the wing mirror and saw it was safe. 'A drink?' she said quietly to Corkbowl.

Not safe. Black Pat leapt forward. His fur rubbed against the car paintwork, pacing next to her now.

'Donkey see, donkey do.' A carnival of vapours. That enormous canoe of a mouth came over to Esther's ear. 'So don't be an ass.'

She sat still.

'Don't accept an invitation from this donkey, Esther.'

She wouldn't give Black Pat the gratification of acknowledging his orders.

Corkbowl slid owlish eyes in her direction. He said, 'I mean, if you were wanting proof of my social inadequacy . . . or a drink.' Here he was, hating himself as he said, 'And it doesn't have to be from a thermos flask either, in case that makes a difference.' He gave it up absolutely with a sigh. 'For the record, all that should have sounded much more inviting than it actually did. It's a classic example of something fun warping into something pathetic . . . a bit like when . . .' He didn't know.

Corkbowl hesitated. 'Umm, I'm not . . .'

'Compostable?' Black Pat guessed for him. He finished, 'Although yes you are.'

'I'm not having much success in thinking of another classic example,' said Corkbowl, 'but I'm sure there are hundreds, like for instance . . .' No, he didn't have an instance.

Esther watched light stripe the windscreen, disappearing with the shade of the wood and then striping.

'Esther, don't ignore me,' Black Pat said. 'I can't let you ignore me.' The whisper begged against her ear. 'I can't let you.'

Esther snapped her fingers, grinning at Corkbowl with the answer. 'I know a classic example of fun and pathetic.' Her fingers snapped again with the victory of it. 'Crying and dancing at the same time. Wretched.'

'Blimey,' Corkbowl said, 'that is *wretched*.'

Esther said, 'You don't cry when you dance, do you?'

'Of course he does,' said Black Pat, disgusted by Corkbowl.

'Not since yesterday,' answered Corkbowl. 'Be serious, Esther,' he said, nearly serious himself, 'I'm too manly to cry, far too manly.' Very sly he added, 'And if you came with me for a drink I could prove it to you. At least, until the music starts.'

'This idiot,' said Black Pat, 'is a revolutionary type of idiot.' He made a crumpled face, sickened. 'He's so idiotic it's radical. I can't – *God* –' A shudder moved across his huge body, then a wet retch. Another retch of rejection, a gassy gagging choke, Esther ignoring him utterly. He shunted away from her window, head forced as if punched back. Black Pat stood there on the road, shrinking with the distance. In the rear-view mirror Esther saw his expression, a bereft one, a forlorn angle to his head. Dejected, he allowed the car to escape.

'It's not often I get invited to go for a drink with a socially inept dancing crier,' Esther said to Corkbowl.

'Didn't think so,' Corkbowl answered. He had this to add: 'Which is lucky, because I was relying on the allure of novelty.'

39

The front door slammed. A precise slam, it was a signal. The hall filled with expectant silence. Conspicuously empty, the house was taut. Esther sidled to the front room. Evidence of Black Pat was everywhere – a sofa cushion thrown off and shaken around the floor, the sofa shoved from the wall, a frayed newspaper, a stick methodically snapped into sections and then chewed at. In the middle of the room she put her bag on the carpet and felt the calmness of nostalgia. She pulled the corduroy cushion back on to the sofa; she piled the shredded newspaper with her feet. She kicked the ruined stick and then left it as a job to do later. He would be here soon. She started for the kitchen.

'You were a while.'

On elbows and stomach he bumped out from behind the sofa and was lying there behind her, his face buried in her bag. A crunch. His hidden jaws worked. She was trying to conceal her mood with all the same behaviour but Black Pat sensed Esther was remote from him. For a moment they were both strange to each other, a frost of unfamiliarity over them.

'The drive took longer than expected,' Esther answered. 'The traffic was quite bad.'

Black Pat's chewing face emerged. 'You didn't go for a drink?' He said this and something shiny dropped from his mouth, then a piece of red plastic. His voice was carefully bored.

'No, we weren't going to go today, just one day in a week or so.

It's only an idea.' She realized she was apologizing. 'Have you eaten my pocket mirror?' She said it as a casual observation. It was the wrong reaction, a confirmation. Black Pat responded with determined destruction, very active in his annihilation of a paperback book pulled from the bag. The paperback was butchered into several smaller ones and then violently enjoyed.

This was reasonably annoying, the book only half read. She took a step forwards and Black Pat's eating became faster, becoming gobbling, relieved to have annoyed her. She took another small step. He gobbled in victory, a jabbering narration coming with it: *Hab-ab-ab-ab-ab! Hab-ab!*

Esther strode towards him and Black Pat wasn't lying on the floor any more. Now he was braced against the floor, ready to leap. The silk lining of her bag was liberated at one corner. Strong jerks persuaded it free with a loud tearing sound. Esther reached for the bag and Black Pat snatched himself away, gobbling great holes in the leather. Lowered into his bracing sprawl he waited for a chase. Black Pat tightened his legs, about to bounce off in escape. In this position he pretended to be uninterested. The end of his tail hovered in hysterical anticipation and ruined the illusion.

Esther stopped the game, surrendering.

Down sagged the tail as she left the room, leaving her bag to be sacrificed. Black Pat's neck rose in a straight stare, ears low and then lifted as he heard her walk to the kitchen. He listened with his ears pitched up, the tips in hard points. He stood quickly and listened. He paced out to the kitchen and his foot caught in the bag, emptying its contents in a trailing mess.

Esther was pouring boiling water into a teapot. She turned and Black Pat was standing in the doorway. On hind legs he rested a shoulder on the wall, his size filling the space. He watched her with a sloped head, his head and shoulder leant against the doorframe. She moved around the kitchen, fetching the milk, fetching two cups.

Black Pat's yellow eyes went with her, examining the shape underneath the clothes. He knew the curve of Esther's knees with those delicate ligaments, relished the swell of her skull; bones in her elbows and wrists were a hymn to him, that network of veins in her feet a poem of circulation. The lust of custody lingered on the cartilage of her ears, on the skin of her neck. Esther fished the tea leaves around with a spoon and his eyes waited. He pressed his head to the door-frame and stared with exploitative patience, his patient waiting a savage assault.

'I've eaten part of your bag,' Black Pat said, slightly hopeful, slightly provocative. 'Most of it actually.'

'It's okay,' she replied, her mildness making dread spring in his chest. 'I've got others.'

'Where?' Black Pat demanded.

She didn't answer, busy stirring a teaspoon. She felt him watch with his jealous eyes.

Black Pat's sloped head stayed against the doorway in its magazine pose. A complex silence ran with undertones.

Esther's cheeks blazed as she poured out a cup of tea. She forced herself to speak with cheerful innocence. 'Do you want one?'

Black Pat didn't, wanting something else. What he wanted sang out in the language of his massive bestial body. That animal physicality resonated through the kitchen with its wild driving appetites and its brutal passion.

Esther sat on the counter, the Formica warm through her skirt. She swung her heels against the cupboards and it was a clumsy disguise. The cause for their strange reserve, for her awkwardness, made a coward of her. Esther stuck to her mute act, heels thumping and placid on the cupboards, just a woman relaxed in her kitchen. But Black Pat could smell the adrenalin reactions in her system. He examined this hormonal recipe and knew the truth.

'Are you all right?' Esther eventually asked. 'You seem a bit –'

'Philosophical? Yes, philosophical.'

No, this was wrong. Esther didn't correct him. 'Is there a particular reason?'

Black Pat gave her a lingering look. '. . . Acutely.'

Esther swallowed a big mouthful of tea. 'Me?'

Black Pat answered no in a way which wasn't. 'I don't like Corkbowl.'

'That's extremely obvious,' said Esther.

'I'm liking him less.' Black Pat mooched down at his hind legs and the floor. 'Less and less. Less than less.'

Esther said cautiously, 'You want to talk about Corkbowl?' She put the cup on the counter and blew on her fingers.

'You know what I want to talk about.'

A silly performance of denial from Esther: 'I don't.'

This started a stand-off between them. A breeze came from the open back door, a breath from the oven of the evening and muggy. Under her fringe her forehead felt damp. She took a clip from her pocket and pinned the fringe up in a weird tuft, trying to end the quarrel. She expected him to ridicule the tuft, wishing for it. With slightly raised eyebrows she saw Black Pat's face sober, the tuft ignored. His sober face became sullen, the look of a heartbreaker scandalized to find himself spurned.

'Please don't,' he said to Esther.

So it had begun. She gave long enough to pretend at confusion. 'Do what?'

'Let me stay.'

A heavy, uncertain stare from Esther. Above the orange light and the chaos of heat the kitchen grew a thin sadness, the empty sadness of a dying relationship. Here it was unstoppably. Black Pat fawned his chops against the wall with a moan.

Esther said, 'Sorry?'

That old Romeo, what he said next was shameless. He said it slowly and full of clues. 'If you let me love you it will be the longest love of your life.'

'You love me?' Esther was shocked to hear her own voice, immediately doubting she had heard him right. As a grotesque experiment she said, 'Black Pat, you don't love me.'

The answer was brazen: 'Oh yes I do.'

'I'm not sure it is love.' She was shy talking like this. A shy little explanation came. 'Because I've had love and I remember how it was.'

'Double it,' said Black Pat. 'Double it, double it. You've got no idea . . . It's a love with a capacity you have no concept of.' Black Pat said with a hot voice, 'It's a love that would endure beyond the precincts of your days with a ferocity you can't hope to equal.'

'Wait . . . ferocity?'

'Boundless, endless, friendless ferocity.'

'No,' Esther said after a speechless period, her eyes dark holes. 'That's not love, it's possession. It's what you did to Michael, you possessed him.'

'I was loyal to him, devoted,' countered Black Pat. The words came through an unusual smile, 'And I'm devoted to you.' The desire was alcoholic, making him teasing. He hammered a paw to his chest. 'I'm devoted. Esther, this . . .' his paw pounded at the chest in demonstration, ' . . . this is devotion.' That coaxing, the animal masculinity of him, they urged her relentlessly. 'Come on,' Black Pat pleaded, 'I'm here now, Esther. Let me stay.'

A great drowsiness, it was the lull of submission, a call from the elephant graveyard of defeat. Then let it take me, thought Esther. She started her weary response and something caused it to lodge unspoken. There was an obstacle, a block stationed in the road. Churchill, with his defiant speech; the agony of Michael; the barracks of Beth and Big Oliver; and Corkbowl, a little light on the shoreline: these sums equated and rose up in a fist of indignant survival. It wasn't a question when she asked, 'Did you ask Michael if you could stay?'

'It was different with Michael, a different arrangement.' Black Pat made a small noncommittal shrug, not wanting to get into this subject. 'He didn't have an option. Neither did Churchill. Because there's not always an option. I was built into the fibre of their lives in a way I'm not . . .' He deliberated. 'With you I'm not as . . .' Black Pat smashed through the finer details, '. . . I'm not immersed in you in the same innate sense.' He added smoothly, 'At this point I'm not, not yet.'

'Which means at this point I have an option as to whether you immerse yourself?'

'Immerse . . . ahm.' He didn't like the term, needing a better word. 'Immerse . . .' He searched for a less menacing word. 'It's more mutual –'

Esther wasn't interested in his horrific jargon. 'I have an option though, don't I?'

'Right now you do.' Honestly he said this, the honesty problematic for him. 'For a while you do. But it decreases and will pass.'

'It will become difficult?'

A convulsed flash of emotion: 'It will become easier.' Persuasive now: 'Esther, it's the easiest thing in the world.'

Esther looked around her at the kitchen, at the wreckage made by Black Pat. Shed fur lined the edges of the cabinets, chips in the veneer made by claws. Dry leaves and sticks in some places, and there a piece of broken glass. Soil and sand streaked across the tiles, tracking into the rest of the house, where patches of paint on the walls were grubbed with dirt. The shreds of material in each room, the mess of chewed wood. A door knocked from its hinges, the pervasive smell. A sheep's pelvis splintered on the landing and then merrily dumped; the cemetery of her garden strewn with small skeletons, the lawn worn to sand. And then she thought of the irresistible advance, his steady progression through the rooms, up the stairs, the distance between them obliterated in five days. Just five days. So imagine what he could do in ten days, in a month, in a lifetime of campaigns. Her hair was in the voluminous style that occurs when hair is continually swept back with sweaty palms, the scalp also sweating.

Black Pat was speaking. 'Believe me, it's easy.' He explained it to her: it was similar to the seduction of sleep. If she stopped resisting it would take her in a lapsing opiate, a painless embrace. She focused on him as he said, 'Esther –' he was beseeching her – 'Esther, all you have to do is consent.'

'Consent to the descent.' She used a toneless whisper. She repeated it to them both.

Black Pat ground his vexed teeth. That enraging, thwarting phrase. He dug his claws into the wallpaper as Esther listened to her memory:

'It's not all you'll have heard': Churchill warning her. 'You are at war . . . On that you must trust me': his warnings were buzzing propeller blades in an amp full of water. They played again.

Black Pat saw her expression, understood it. 'Please . . . please, Esther . . .'

She wasn't angry or demanding, she was unemotional as she said, 'I can't consent.'

'No, this is a transitional –'

Her interruption was gentle. 'No, this is our goodbye.' Before he could argue she said, 'I've realized I owe it to myself.' A pause. 'Black Pat, this is goodbye.'

'You've realized you owe yourself? You realized alone?' Black Pat wore a resentful smile. It softened, it didn't matter. 'That prune Corkbowl didn't exactly help. Neither did Churchill.' He considered smirking. Too morose, he couldn't. 'You three formed a sort of trinity of idiots and made a resistance against me.'

Esther grinned at her knees. 'A trinity of idiots? As glamorous as that?'

'Not really.' His confession, it came with a sigh. 'In fairness you resisted quite well on your own.' A moment passed in silence. 'I thought I had you.'

'Perhaps for a bit,' she answered. 'Perhaps for a while.'

'I did, didn't I?'

'You were very close.'

'More than close.' Black Pat's tone was soulful. 'I was sure I had you.'

'So was I, for what it's worth.'

'It's not worth a dime.'

Esther recalled their first meeting. 'Not a thousand pounds?' The answer was obvious, she said it anyway, 'You don't pay though, do you?'

'Only one of us would have ever paid.' He watched her with those lonely eyes. 'And I can't take anything less than everything.'

Esther sat there on the counter. She linked her ankles.

'Well . . .' Black Pat pretended at acceptance, a handsome effort, ' . . . you win some, you lose some. You skin some, you bruise some. You tin some, you juice some.' He scraped the fur on his chin into a neat Vandyke beard. 'That's me quoting myself, I hope you appreciate.'

Esther said, 'You almost won.' She was bashful as she told him, 'And to quote you, it would have been the easiest thing in the world.'

'It's either my way or the hard way.' Then Black Pat clicked his gums, acknowledging the con. 'But in truth, in time, my way is the hardest way imaginable.' He stood in the doorway as a minute went by.

'So this is our goodbye.'

An amber haze of late sun fogged the left side of Esther's vision. 'Will you be back?'

'If you're unlucky.'

Her cheek glowed in the sun, the sun over her head and dress in a bronze plate. 'Will I be unlucky?'

'Maybe not.' Black Pat studied her from across the room. He said, '*Tchk*,' at his fond foolishness and then, '*Huff*.' Useless to fight it, he repeated softly, 'Maybe not.'

The sun was in a diagonal band down his hip, down his tail, his face in shade.

'Maybe not.' Esther was satisfied enough.

Black Pat's parting, he gave her a wink. '. . . Esther, I hope not.'

Another wink, a wink of farewell. He was gone.

Monday 27 July 1964

40

11.15 a.m.

In the office Churchill was stationary, his pinstriped trousers two masts below the rotund buoy of his stomach. The Romeo y Julieta cigar was still in his hand and he took in a mouthful of smoke, held it rolling there, and exhaled it expressively. The smoke made a strong spectral passage through the air, dispersing gently.

He said, 'And so we reach the end.'

Black Pat was at the other end of the room, ears set in peaks.

'Yes,' Churchill said to himself, looking down as he smoothed his shirt, working over it in sweeps. 'Here we are at last.'

Black Pat examined the toes of his front paws. The knuckles were defined through the fur, sketching the giant skeleton within. 'We don't have long.'

'I know.'

'Did you expect it to be different?'

'How could I?' Churchill skewed a glance at him. 'What possibility was there that it could ever be different?'

Black Pat answered, the words released gradually, 'I suppose there's always a slim chance.'

'Incorrigible liar,' Churchill said, his expression of weary good humour.

Moving over to a cabinet, Churchill bent to stare into it. He retrieved a bottle of Pol Roger champagne and lifted it affectionately, admiring its curving neck. The dog had dropped into a crouch, muscles in his legs stretched to combust in an explosion of energy as Churchill eased the cork, teasing it free. It popped and shot across the room.

Ready, Black Pat launched, the cork caught in his mouth and milled apart with loud teeth.

A crystal effervescent sound was in the room as Churchill filled a glass. 'You were always good at that.'

'Years of practice.' Black Pat grinned, granules of cork sprinkling over the floor.

Churchill rotated his glass, bubbles rallying in chains to the surface. The sky outside strummed with the promise of long, hot hours tapering into a light and tropical evening.

They stayed quietly for a while, a complicated harmony between them.

Black Pat sat down, eventually speaking. 'That I have to be with you at this moment,' he hesitated with a glottal noise, 'is something I regret . . .'

Churchill sipped his drink. 'What a curious bloody oddity you are.'

Black Pat laughed in a grunt, the released note like air blown over the lip of a bottle. 'But I am obliged to accompany you through this. It is an obligation, not a choice.'

Churchill walked across the room. 'Yes, I understand. We have to honour our commitments and be steadfast, all of us.'

At the window he watched birds in the plane tree, sparrows darting between branches with tiny wingbeats, bickering and busy in a fleeting microcosm.

'You remember the Churchill family motto, don't you?' he said into the window glass, his reflection on it. 'Fiel pero desdichado: Faithful but unfortunate.'

Churchill's head turned to talk to Black Pat over a shoulder, his head held there momentarily. 'Sums us up perfectly.'

' . . . We have to go.'

A thought came to Churchill, a smile with the potency of milk coming with it. 'Perhaps a revision is in order; Fiel sin importar pura animosidad: Faithful regardless of pure animosity.'

Fingertips made brief contact with the bridge of his nose, the smile evaporating from the reflection. 'Oh, but I don't say this with any conviction. You are a dark star in the constellation which forms me. And to fight against you is to try and fight the stars in the eternal firmament.'

Black Pat spoke softly, getting up. 'If I could leave you now, if this was something in my power, I would do it.'

Churchill turned from the sparrows and their plane-tree universe, answering in a sigh. 'Pah, it's not your fault, you old gooseberry. Neither of us can break this contract.'

Black Pat stood in the centre of the room, a ghoul with watchful eyes. 'It's time. Are you ready?'

'Very nearly,' Churchill answered. 'Forgive me if I take one more minute.' The cigar had fumbled itself out. Making a quick assessment he lit it, producing more clouds.

The dog's voice came again. 'Are you ready?'

Churchill took his strength in great handfuls, prepared to go to the press conference, prepared for the end of the beginning. 'Yes, I am ready now.'

Black Pat padded to Churchill's side, tail brushing his hind legs.

Churchill's hand found the doorknob. The door pushed open. His next command was for them both. 'So then, onwards.'